Charlie and the Chocolate Factory

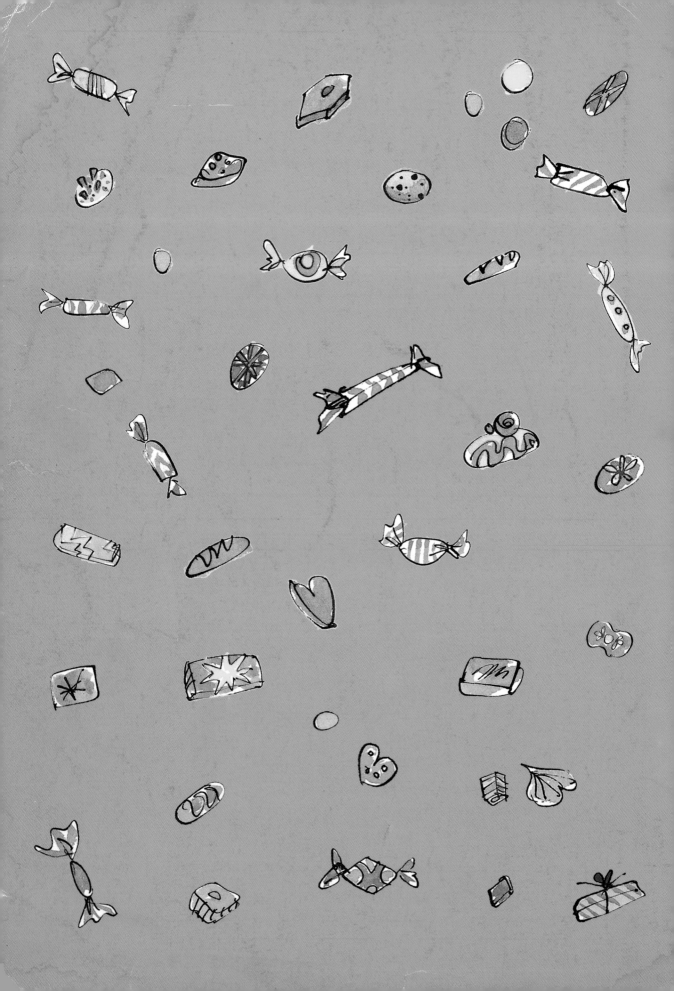

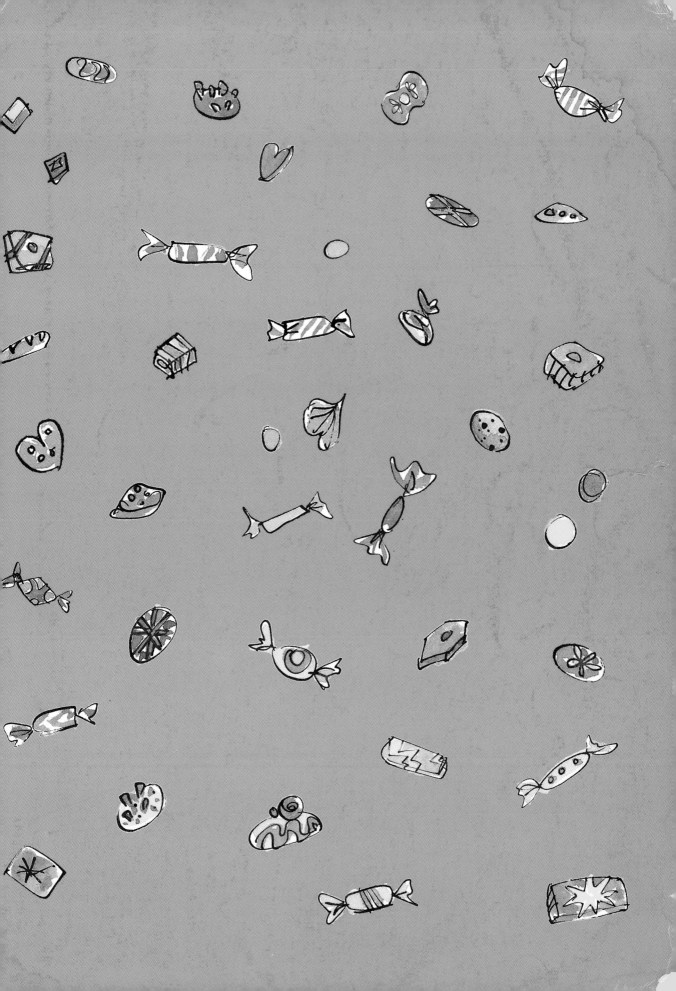

THIS BOOK BELONGS TO

....

Find out more about Roald Dahl
by visiting the Web site at
www.roalddahl.com.

This book is for Olivia and Tessa

PUFFIN BOOKS
Published by the Penguin Group
Penguin Young Readers Group, 345 Hudson Street, New York, New York 10014, U.S.A.
Penguin Group (Canada), 90 Eglinton Avenue East, Suite 700, Toronto, Ontario, Canada M4P 2Y3
(a division of Pearson Penguin Canada Inc.)
Penguin Books Ltd, 80 Strand, London WC2R 0RL, England
Penguin Ireland, 25 St Stephen's Green, Dublin 2, Ireland (a division of Penguin Books Ltd)
Penguin Group (Australia), 250 Camberwell Road, Camberwell, Victoria 3124, Australia
(a division of Pearson Australia Group Pty Ltd)
Penguin Books India Pvt Ltd, 11 Community Centre, Panchsheel Park, New Delhi – 110 017, India
Penguin Group (NZ), 67 Apollo Drive, Rosedale, North Shore 0632, New Zealand
(a division of Pearson New Zealand Ltd)
Penguin Books (South Africa) (Pty) Ltd, 24 Sturdee Avenue, Rosebank, Johannesburg 2196, South Africa

Registered Offices: Penguin Books Ltd, 80 Strand, London WC2R 0RL, England

First published in the United States of America, 1964
First published in Great Britain by George Allen & Unwin, 1967
Published in Puffin Books, 1973
Color edition first published by Viking, 1997
Published by Puffin Books, 2004
This edition published by Puffin Books, a division of Penguin Young Readers Group, 2011

1 3 5 7 9 10 8 6 4 2

Text copyright © Roald Dahl Nominee Ltd, 1964
Illustrations copyright © Quentin Blake, 1995, 1997
Color treatment by Vida Williams
The moral right of the illustrator has been asserted
All rights reserved
Text set in Bembo and QuentinBlake

Puffin Books ISBN 978-0-14-241821-5

Manufactured in China

ROALD DAHL

ILLUSTRATED BY QUENTIN BLAKE

Charlie and the Chocolate Factory

PUFFIN BOOKS
An Imprint of Penguin Group (USA) Inc.

Contents

There are five children in this book:

AUGUSTUS GLOOP
A greedy boy

VERUCA SALT
A girl who is spoiled by her parents

VIOLET BEAUREGARDE
A girl who chews gum all day long

MIKE TEAVEE
A boy who does nothing but watch television

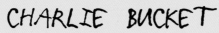

and

CHARLIE BUCKET
The hero

CHAPTER ONE

Here Comes Charlie

These two very old people are the father and mother of Mr. Bucket. Their names are Grandpa Joe and Grandma Josephine.

And *these* two very old people are the father and mother of Mrs. Bucket. Their names are Grandpa George and Grandma Georgina.

This is Mr. Bucket. This is Mrs. Bucket.

Mr. and Mrs. Bucket have a small boy whose name is Charlie Bucket.

This is Charlie.

How d'you do? And how d'you do? And how d'you do again?

He is pleased to meet you.

The whole of this family—the six grown-ups (count them) and little Charlie Bucket—live together in a small wooden house on the edge of a great town.

The house wasn't nearly large enough for so many people, and life was extremely uncomfortable for them all. There were only two rooms in the place altogether, and there was only one bed. The bed was given to the four old grandparents because they were so old and tired. They were so tired, they never got out of it.

Grandpa Joe and Grandma Josephine on this side, Grandpa George and Grandma Georgina on this side.

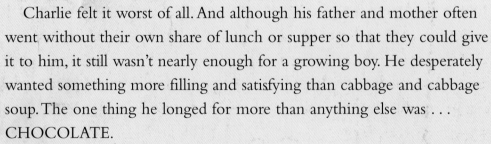

Mr. and Mrs. Bucket and little Charlie Bucket slept in the other room, upon mattresses on the floor.

In the summertime, this wasn't too bad, but in the winter, freezing cold drafts blew across the floor all night long, and it was awful.

There wasn't any question of them being able to buy a better house—or even one more bed to sleep in. They were far too poor for that.

Mr. Bucket was the only person in the family with a job. He worked in a toothpaste factory, where he sat all day long at a bench and screwed the little caps on to the tops of the tubes of toothpaste after the tubes had been filled. But a toothpaste cap-screwer is never paid very much money, and poor Mr. Bucket, however hard he worked, and however fast he screwed on the caps, was never able to make enough to buy one half of the things that so large a family needed. There wasn't even enough money to buy proper food for them all. The only meals they could afford were bread and margarine for breakfast, boiled potatoes and cabbage for lunch, and cabbage soup for supper. Sundays were a bit better. They all looked forward to Sundays because then, although they had exactly the same, everyone was allowed a second helping.

The Buckets, of course, didn't starve, but every one of them—the two old grandfathers, the two old grandmothers, Charlie's father, Charlie's mother, and especially little Charlie himself—went about from morning till night with a horrible empty feeling in their tummies.

Charlie felt it worst of all. And although his father and mother often went without their own share of lunch or supper so that they could give it to him, it still wasn't nearly enough for a growing boy. He desperately wanted something more filling and satisfying than cabbage and cabbage soup. The one thing he longed for more than anything else was . . . CHOCOLATE.

Walking to school in the mornings, Charlie could see great slabs of chocolate piled up high in the shop windows, and he would stop and stare and press his nose against the glass, his mouth watering like mad.

Many times a day, he would see other children taking bars of creamy chocolate out of their pockets and munching them greedily, and *that*, of course, was *pure* torture.

Only once a year, on his birthday, did Charlie Bucket ever get to taste a bit of chocolate. The whole family saved up their money for that special occasion, and when the great day arrived, Charlie was always presented with one small chocolate bar to eat all by himself. And each time he received it, on those marvelous birthday mornings, he would place it carefully in a small wooden box that he owned, and treasure it as though it were a bar of solid gold; and for the next few days, he would

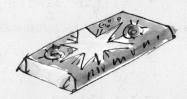

allow himself only to look at it, but never to touch it. Then at last, when he could stand it no longer, he would peel back a *tiny* bit of the paper wrapping at one corner to expose a *tiny* bit of chocolate, and then he would take a *tiny* nibble–just enough to allow the lovely sweet taste to spread out slowly over his tongue. The next day, he would take another tiny nibble, and so on, and so on. And in this way, Charlie would make his sixpenny bar of birthday chocolate last him for more than a month.

But I haven't yet told you about the one awful thing that tortured little Charlie, the lover of chocolate, more than *anything* else. This thing, for him, was far, far worse than seeing slabs of chocolate in the shop windows or watching other children munching bars of creamy chocolate right in front of him. It was the most terrible torturing thing you could imagine, and it was this:

In the town itself, actually within *sight* of the house in which Charlie lived, there was an ENORMOUS CHOCOLATE FACTORY!

Just imagine that!

Charlie and the Chocolate Factory

And it wasn't simply an ordinary enormous chocolate factory, either.
It was the largest and most famous in the whole world! It was
WONKA'S FACTORY, owned by a man called Mr. Willy Wonka, the
greatest inventor and maker of chocolates that there has ever been.
And what a tremendous, marvelous place it was! It had huge iron gates
leading into it, and a high wall surrounding it, and smoke belching from
its chimneys, and strange whizzing sounds coming from deep inside it.
And outside the walls, for half a mile around in every direction, the air
was scented with the heavy rich smell of melting chocolate!

Twice a day, on his way to and from school, little Charlie Bucket had
to walk right past the gates of the factory. And every time he went by, he
would begin to walk very, very slowly, and he would hold his nose high
in the air and take long deep sniffs of the gorgeous chocolatey smell all
around him.

Oh, how he loved that smell!

And oh, how he wished he could go inside the factory and see what
it was like!

CHAPTER TWO
Mr. Willy Wonka's Factory

In the evenings, after he had finished his supper of watery cabbage soup, Charlie always went into the room of his four grandparents to listen to their stories, and then afterwards to say good night.

Every one of these old people was over ninety. They were as shriveled as prunes, and as bony as skeletons, and throughout the day, until Charlie made his appearance, they lay huddled in their one bed, two at either end, with nightcaps on to keep their heads warm, dozing the time away with nothing to do. But as soon as they heard the door opening, and heard Charlie's voice saying, "Good evening, Grandpa Joe and Grandma Josephine, and Grandpa George and Grandma Georgina," then all four of them would suddenly sit up, and their old wrinkled faces would light up with smiles of pleasure–and the talking would begin. For they loved this little boy. He was the only bright thing in their lives, and his evening visits were something that they looked forward to all day long. Often, Charlie's mother and father would come in as well, and stand by the door, listening to the stories that the old people told; and thus, for perhaps half an hour every night, this room would become a happy place, and the whole family would forget that it was hungry and poor.

One evening, when Charlie went in to see his grandparents, he said to them, "Is it *really* true that Wonka's Chocolate Factory is the biggest in the world?"

"*True?*" cried all four of them at once. "Of course it's true! Good heavens, didn't you know *that*? It's about *fifty* times as big as any other!"

"And is Mr. Willy Wonka *really* the cleverest chocolate maker in the world?"

"My *dear* boy," said Grandpa Joe, raising himself up a little higher on his pillow, "Mr. Willy Wonka is the most *amazing*, the most *fantastic*, the most *extraordinary* chocolate maker the world has ever seen! I thought *everybody* knew that!"

"I knew he was famous, Grandpa Joe, and I knew he was very clever . . ."

"*Clever!*" cried the old man. "He's more than that! He's a *magician* with chocolate! He can make *anything*–anything he wants! Isn't that a fact, my dears?"

The other three old people nodded their heads slowly up and down, and said, "*Absolutely* true. *Just* as true as can be."

And Grandpa Joe said, "You mean to say I've never *told* you about Mr. Willy Wonka and his factory?"

"Never," answered little Charlie.

"Good heavens above! I don't know what's the matter with me!"

"Will you tell me now, Grandpa Joe, please?"

"I certainly will. Sit down beside me on the bed, my dear, and listen carefully."

Grandpa Joe was the oldest of the four grandparents. He was ninety-six and a half, and that is just about as old as anybody can be. Like all extremely old people, he was delicate and weak, and throughout the day he spoke very little. But in the evenings, when Charlie, his beloved grandson, was in the room, he seemed in some marvelous way to grow quite young again. All his tiredness fell away from him, and he became as eager and excited as a young boy.

"Oh, what a man he is, this Mr. Willy Wonka!" cried Grandpa Joe. "Did you know, for example, that he has himself invented more than two hundred new kinds of chocolate bars, each with a different center, each far sweeter and creamier and more delicious than anything the other chocolate factories can make!"

"Perfectly true!" cried Grandma Josephine. "And he sends them to *all* the four corners of the earth! Isn't that so, Grandpa Joe?"

"It is, my dear, it is. And to all the kings and presidents of the world as well. But it isn't only chocolate bars that he makes. Oh, dear me, no! He has some really *fantastic* inventions up his sleeve, Mr. Willy Wonka has! Did you know that he's invented a way of making chocolate ice cream so that it stays cold for hours and hours without being in the refrigerator? You can even leave it lying in the sun all morning on a hot day and it won't go runny!"

"But that's *impossible*!" said little Charlie, staring at his grandfather.

"Of course it's impossible!" cried Grandpa Joe. "It's completely *absurd*! But Mr. Willy Wonka has done it!"

"Quite right!" the others agreed, nodding their heads. "Mr. Wonka has done it."

"And then again," Grandpa Joe went on speaking very slowly now so that Charlie wouldn't miss a word, "Mr. Willy Wonka can make marshmallows that taste of violets, and rich caramels that change color every ten seconds as you suck them, and little feathery sweets that melt away deliciously the moment you put them between your lips. He can make chewing-gum that never loses its taste, and sugar balloons that you can blow up to enormous sizes before you pop them with a pin and gobble them up. And, by a most secret method, he can make lovely blue birds' eggs with black spots on them, and when you put one of these in your mouth, it gradually gets smaller and smaller until suddenly there is nothing left except a tiny little pink sugary baby bird sitting on the tip of your tongue."

Grandpa Joe paused and ran the point of his tongue slowly over his lips. "It makes my mouth water just *thinking* about it," he said.

"Mine, too," said little Charlie. "But *please* go on."

While they were talking, Mr. and Mrs. Bucket, Charlie's mother and father, had come quietly into the room, and now both were standing just inside the door, listening.

"Tell Charlie about that crazy Indian prince," said Grandma Josephine. "He'd like to hear that."

"You mean Prince Pondicherry?" said Grandpa Joe, and he began chuckling with laughter.

"*Completely* dotty!" said Grandpa George.

"But *very* rich," said Grandma Georgina.

"What did he do?" asked Charlie eagerly.

"Listen," said Grandpa Joe, "and I'll tell you."

CHAPTER THREE

Mr. Wonka and the Indian Prince

"Prince Pondicherry wrote a letter to Mr. Willy Wonka," said Grandpa Joe, "and asked him to come all the way out to India and build him a colossal palace entirely out of chocolate."

"Did Mr. Wonka do it, Grandpa?"

"He did, indeed. And what a palace it was! It had one hundred rooms, and *everything* was made of either dark or light chocolate! The bricks were chocolate, and the cement holding them together was chocolate, and the windows were chocolate, and all the walls and ceilings were made of chocolate, so were the carpets and the pictures and the furniture and the beds; and when you turned on the taps in the bathroom, hot chocolate came pouring out.

"When it was all finished, Mr. Wonka said to Prince Pondicherry, 'I warn you, though, it won't last very long, so you'd better start eating it right away.'

" 'Nonsense!' shouted the Prince. 'I'm not going to eat my palace! I'm not even going to nibble the staircase or lick the walls! I'm going to *live* in it!'

"But Mr. Wonka was right, of course, because soon after this, there came a very hot day with a boiling sun, and the whole palace began to melt, and then it sank slowly to the ground, and the crazy prince, who was dozing in the living room at the time, woke up to find himself swimming around in a huge brown sticky lake of chocolate."

Little Charlie sat very still on the edge of the bed, staring at his grandfather.

Charlie's face was bright, and his eyes were stretched so wide you could see the whites all around. "Is all this *really* true?" he asked. "Or are you pulling my leg?"

"It's true!" cried all four of the old people at once. "Of course it's true! Ask anyone you like!"

"And I'll tell you something else that's true," said Grandpa Joe, and now he leaned closer to Charlie, and lowered his voice to a soft, secret whisper. "*Nobody . . . ever . . . comes . . . out!*"

"Out of where?" asked Charlie.

"*And . . . nobody . . . ever . . . goes . . . in!*"

"In *where*?" cried Charlie.

"Wonka's factory, of course!"

"Grandpa, what *do* you mean?"

"I mean *workers*, Charlie."

"Workers?"

"All factories," said Grandpa Joe, "have workers streaming in and out of the gates in the mornings and evenings–except Wonka's! Have *you* ever seen a single person going into that place–or coming out?"

Little Charlie looked slowly around at each of the four old faces, one after the other, and they all looked back at him. They were friendly smiling faces, but they were also quite serious. There was no sign of joking or leg-pulling on any of them.

"Well? Have *you*?" asked Grandpa Joe.

"I . . . I really don't know, Grandpa," Charlie stammered. "Whenever I walk past the factory, the gates seem to be closed."

"Exactly!" said Grandpa Joe.

"But there *must* be people working there . . ."

"Not *people*, Charlie. Not *ordinary* people, anyway."

"Then who?" cried Charlie.

"Ah-ha . . . That's it, you see . . . That's another of Mr. Willy Wonka's clevernesses."

"Charlie, dear," Mrs. Bucket called out from where she was standing by the door, "it's time for bed. That's enough for tonight."

"But, Mother, I *must* hear . . ."

"Tomorrow, my darling . . ."

"That's right," said Grandpa Joe, "I'll tell you the rest of it tomorrow evening."

CHAPTER FOUR

The Secret Workers

The next evening, Grandpa Joe went on with his story.

"You see, Charlie," he said, "not so very long ago there used to be thousands of people working in Mr. Willy Wonka's factory. Then one day, all of a sudden, Mr. Wonka had to ask *every single one of them* to leave, to go home, never to come back."

"But why?" asked Charlie.

"Because of spies."

"Spies?"

"Yes. All the other chocolate makers, you see, had begun to grow jealous of the wonderful sweets that Mr. Wonka was making, and they started sending in spies to steal his secret recipes. The spies took jobs in the Wonka factory, pretending that they were ordinary workers, and while they were there, each one of them found out exactly how a certain special thing was made."

"And did they go back to their own factories and tell?" asked Charlie.

"They must have," answered Grandpa Joe, "because soon after that, Fickelgruber's factory started making an ice cream that would never melt, even in the hottest sun. Then Mr. Prodnose's factory came out with a chewing-gum that never lost its flavor however much you chewed it. And then Mr. Slugworth's factory began making sugar balloons that you could blow up to huge sizes before you popped them with a pin and gobbled them up. And so on, and so on. And Mr. Willy Wonka tore his beard and shouted, 'This is terrible! I shall be ruined! There are spies everywhere! I shall have to close the factory!' "

"But he didn't do that!" Charlie said.

"Oh, yes he did. He told *all* the workers that he was sorry, but they would have to go home. Then, he shut the main gates and fastened them with a chain. And suddenly, Wonka's giant chocolate factory became silent and deserted. The chimneys stopped smoking, the machines stopped whirring, and from then on, not a single chocolate or sweet was made. Not a soul went in or out, and even Mr. Willy Wonka himself disappeared completely.

"Months and months went by," Grandpa Joe went on, "but still the factory remained closed. And everybody said, "Poor Mr. Wonka. He was so nice. And he made such marvelous things. But he's finished now. It's all over."

"Then something astonishing happened. One day, early in the morning, thin columns of white smoke were seen to be coming out of the tops of the tall chimneys of the factory! People in the town stopped and stared. 'What's going on?' they cried. 'Someone's lit the furnaces! Mr. Wonka must be opening up again!' They ran to the gates, expecting to

see them wide open and Mr. Wonka standing there to welcome his workers back.

"But no! The great iron gates were still locked and chained as securely as ever, and Mr. Wonka was nowhere to be seen.

" 'But the factory *is* working!' the people shouted. 'Listen! You can hear the machines! They're all whirring again! And you can smell the smell of melting chocolate in the air!' "

Grandpa Joe leaned forward and laid a long bony finger on Charlie's knee, and he said softly, "But most mysterious of all, Charlie, were the shadows in the windows of the factory. The people standing on the street outside could see small dark shadows moving about behind the frosted glass windows."

"Shadows of whom?" said Charlie quickly.

"That's exactly what everybody else wanted to know.

" 'The place is full of workers!' the people shouted. 'But nobody's gone in! The gates are locked! It's crazy! Nobody ever comes out, either!'

"But there was no question at all," said Grandpa Joe, "that the factory was running. And it's gone on running ever since, for these last ten years. What's more, the chocolates and sweets it's been turning out have become more fantastic and delicious all the time. And of course now when Mr. Wonka invents some new and wonderful sweet, neither Mr. Fickelgruber nor Mr. Prodnose nor Mr. Slugworth nor anybody else is able to copy it. No spies can go into the factory to find out how it is made."

"But Grandpa, *who*," cried Charlie, "*who* is Mr. Wonka using to do all the work in the factory?"

"Nobody knows, Charlie."

"But that's *absurd*! Hasn't someone asked Mr. Wonka?"

"Nobody sees him any more. He never comes out. The only things that come out of that place are chocolates and sweets. They come out through a special trap door in the wall, all packed and addressed, and they are picked up every day by Post Office trucks."

"But Grandpa, what *sort* of people are they that work in there?"

"My dear boy," said Grandpa Joe, "that is one of the great mysteries of the chocolate-making world. We know only one thing about them. They are very small. The faint shadows that sometimes appear behind the windows, especially late at night when the lights are on, are those of *tiny* people, people no taller than my knee . . ."

"There aren't any such people," Charlie said.

Just then, Mr. Bucket, Charlie's father, came into the room. He was home from the toothpaste factory, and he was waving an evening newspaper rather excitedly. "Have you heard the news?" he cried. He held up the paper so that they could see the huge headline. The headline said:

WONKA FACTORY TO BE OPENED AT LAST TO LUCKY FEW

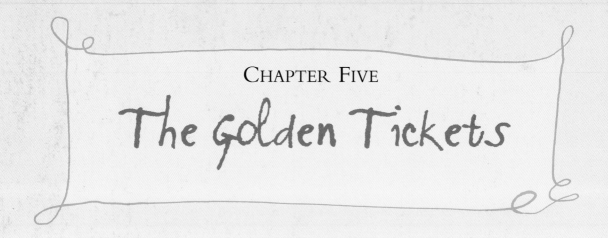

CHAPTER FIVE

The Golden Tickets

"You mean people are actually going to be allowed to go inside the factory?" cried Grandpa Joe. "Read us what it says—quickly!"

"All right," said Mr. Bucket, smoothing out the newspaper. "Listen."

Evening Bulletin

Mr. Willy Wonka, the confectionery genius whom nobody has seen for the last ten years, sent out the following notice today:

I, Willy Wonka, have decided to allow five children—just *five*, mind you, and no more—to visit my factory this year. These lucky five will be shown around personally by me, and they will be allowed to see all the secrets and the magic of my factory. Then, at the end of the tour, as a special present, all of them will be given enough chocolates and sweets to last them for the rest of their lives! So watch out for the Golden Tickets! Five Golden Tickets have been printed on golden paper, and these five Golden Tickets have been hidden underneath the ordinary wrapping paper of five ordinary bars of chocolate. These five chocolate bars may be anywhere—in any shop in any street in any town in any country in the world—upon any counter where Wonka's Sweets are sold. And the five lucky finders of these five Golden Tickets are the *only* ones who will be allowed to visit my factory and see what it's like *now* inside! Good luck to you all, and happy hunting! (Signed Willy Wonka.)

The Golden Tickets

"The man's dotty!" muttered Grandma Josephine.

"He's brilliant!" cried Grandpa Joe. "He's a magician! Just imagine what will happen now! The whole world will be searching for those Golden Tickets! Everyone will be buying Wonka's chocolate bars in the hope of finding one! He'll sell more than ever before! Oh, how exciting it would be to find one!"

"And all the chocolate and sweets that you could eat for the rest of your life–*free*!" said Grandpa George. "Just imagine that!"

"They'd have to deliver them in a truck!" said Grandma Georgina.

"It makes me quite ill to think of it," said Grandma Josephine.

"Nonsense!" cried Grandpa Joe. "Wouldn't it be *something*, Charlie, to open a bar of chocolate and see a Golden Ticket glistening inside!"

"It certainly would, Grandpa. But there isn't a hope," Charlie said sadly. "I only get one bar a year."

"You never know, darling," said Grandma Georgina. "It's your birthday next week. You have as much chance as anybody else."

"I'm afraid that simply isn't true," said Grandpa George. "The kids who are going to find the Golden Tickets are the ones who can afford to buy bars of chocolate every day. Our Charlie gets only one a year. There isn't a hope."

CHAPTER SIX
The First Two Finders

The very next day, the first Golden Ticket was found. The finder was a boy called Augustus Gloop, and Mr. Bucket's evening newspaper carried a large picture of him on the front page. The picture showed a nine-year-old boy who was so enormously fat he looked as though he had been blown up with a powerful pump. Great flabby folds of fat bulged out from every part of his body, and his face was like a monstrous ball of dough with two small greedy currant eyes peering out upon the world. The town in which Augustus Gloop lived, the newspaper said, had gone wild with excitement over their hero. Flags were flying from all the windows, children had been given a holiday from school, and a parade was being organized in honor of the famous youth.

"I just *knew* Augustus would find a Golden Ticket," his mother had told the newspapermen. "He eats *so many* bars of chocolate a day that it was almost *impossible* for him *not* to find one. Eating is his hobby, you know. That's *all* he's interested in. But still, that's better than being a *hooligan* and shooting off *zip guns* and things like that in his spare time, isn't it? And what I always say is, he wouldn't go on eating like he does unless he *needed* nourishment, would he? It's all *vitamins*, anyway. What a *thrill* it will be for him to visit Mr. Wonka's marvelous factory! We're just as *proud* as anything!"

"What a revolting woman," said Grandma Josephine.

"And what a repulsive boy," said Grandma Georgina.

"Only four Golden Tickets left," said Grandpa George. "I wonder who'll get *those*."

And now the whole country, indeed,
the whole world, seemed suddenly
to be caught up in a mad
chocolate-buying spree,
everybody searching frantically
for those precious remaining
tickets. Fully grown women
were seen going into sweet
shops and buying ten Wonka
bars at a time, then tearing
off the wrappers on the spot
and peering eagerly
underneath for a glint of
golden paper. Children were
taking hammers and
smashing their piggy banks
and running out to the shops
with handfuls of money. In
one city, a famous gangster
robbed a bank of a thousand pounds
and spent the whole lot on Wonka bars that same afternoon. And when
the police entered his house to arrest him, they found him sitting on the
floor amidst mountains of chocolate, ripping off the wrappers with the
blade of a long dagger. In far-off Russia, a woman called Charlotte Russe
claimed to have found the second ticket, but it turned out to be a clever
fake. The famous English scientist, Professor Foulbody, invented a
machine which would tell you at once, without opening the wrapper of
a bar of chocolate, whether or not there was a Golden Ticket hidden
underneath it. The machine had a mechanical arm that shot out with
tremendous force and grabbed hold of anything that had the slightest bit
of gold inside it, and for a moment, it looked like the answer to

everything. But unfortunately, while the Professor was showing off the machine to the public at the sweet counter of a large department store, the mechanical arm shot out and made a grab for the gold filling in the back tooth of a duchess who was standing near by. There was an ugly scene, and the machine was smashed by the crowd.

Suddenly, on the day before Charlie Bucket's birthday, the newspapers announced that the second Golden Ticket had been found. The lucky person was a small girl called Veruca Salt who lived with her rich parents in a great city far away. Once again Mr. Bucket's evening newspaper carried a big picture of the finder. She was sitting between her beaming father and mother in the living room of their house, waving the Golden Ticket above her head, and grinning from ear to ear.

Veruca's father, Mr. Salt, had eagerly explained to the newspapermen exactly how the ticket was found. "You see, boys," he had said, "as soon as

my little girl told me that she simply *had* to have one of those Golden Tickets, I went out into the town and started buying up all the Wonka bars I could lay my hands on. *Thousands* of them, I must have bought. *Hundreds* of thousands! Then I had them loaded on to trucks and sent directly to my own factory. I'm in the peanut business, you see, and I've got about a hundred women working for me over at my place, shelling peanuts for roasting and salting. That's what they do all day long, those women, they sit there shelling peanuts. So I says to them, 'Okay, girls,' I says, 'from now on, you can stop shelling peanuts and start shelling the wrappers off these chocolate bars instead!' And they did. I had every worker in the place yanking the paper off those bars of chocolate full speed ahead from morning till night.

"But three days went by, and we had no luck. Oh, it was terrible! My little Veruca got more and more upset each day, and every time I went home she would scream at me, '*Where's my Golden Ticket! I want my Golden Ticket!*' And she would lie for hours on the floor, kicking and yelling in the most disturbing way. Well, I just hated to see my little girl feeling unhappy like that, so I vowed I would keep up the search until I'd got her what she wanted. Then suddenly . . . on the evening of the fourth day, one of my women workers yelled, 'I've got it! A Golden Ticket!' And I said, 'Give it to me, quick!' and she did, and I rushed it home and gave it to my darling Veruca, and now she's all smiles, and we have a happy home once again."

"That's even worse than the fat boy," said Grandma Josephine.

"She needs a really good spanking," said Grandma Georgina.

"I don't think the girl's father played it quite fair, Grandpa, do you?" Charlie murmured.

"He spoils her," Grandpa Joe said. "And no good can ever come from spoiling a child like that, Charlie, you mark my words."

"Come to bed, my darling," said Charlie's mother. "Tomorrow's your birthday, don't forget that, so I expect you'll be up early to open your present."

"A Wonka chocolate bar!" cried Charlie. "It is a Wonka bar, isn't it?"

"Yes, my love," his mother said. "Of course it is."

"Oh, wouldn't it be wonderful if I found the third Golden Ticket inside it?" Charlie said.

"Bring it in here when you get it," Grandpa Joe said. "Then we can all watch you taking off the wrapper."

CHAPTER SEVEN
Charlie's Birthday

"Happy birthday!" cried the four old grandparents, as Charlie came into their room early the next morning.

Charlie smiled nervously and sat down on the edge of the bed. He was holding his present, his only present, very carefully in his two hands. WONKA'S WHIPPLE-SCRUMPTIOUS FUDGEMALLOW DELIGHT, it said on the wrapper.

The four old people, two at either end of the bed, propped themselves up on their pillows and stared with anxious eyes at the bar of chocolate in Charlie's hands.

Mr. and Mrs. Bucket came in and stood at the foot of the bed, watching Charlie.

The room became silent. Everybody was waiting now for Charlie to start opening his present. Charlie looked down at the bar of chocolate. He ran his fingers slowly back and forth along the length of it, stroking it lovingly, and the shiny paper wrapper made little sharp crackly noises in the quiet room.

Then Mrs. Bucket said gently, "You mustn't be too disappointed, my darling, if you don't find what you're looking for underneath that wrapper. You really can't expect to be as lucky as all that."

"She's quite right," Mr. Bucket said.

Charlie didn't say anything.

"After all," Grandma Josephine said, "in the whole wide world there are only three tickets left to be found."

"The thing to remember," Grandma Georgina said, "is that whatever happens, you'll still have the bar of chocolate."

"Wonka's Whipple-Scrumptious Fudgemallow Delight!" cried Grandpa George. "It's the best of them all! You'll just *love* it!"

"Yes," Charlie whispered. "I know."

"Just forget all about those Golden Tickets and enjoy the chocolate," Grandpa Joe said. "Why don't you do that?"

They all knew it was ridiculous to expect this one poor little bar of chocolate to have a magic ticket inside it, and they were trying as gently and as kindly as they could to prepare Charlie for the disappointment. But there was one other thing that the grown-ups also knew, and it was this: that however *small* the chance might be of striking lucky, *the chance was there*.

The chance *had* to be there.

This particular bar of chocolate had as much chance as any other of having a Golden Ticket.

And that was why all the grandparents and parents in the room were actually just as tense and excited as Charlie was, although they were pretending to be very calm.

"You'd better go ahead and open it up, or you'll be late for school," Grandpa Joe said.

Charlie's Birthday

"You might as well get it over with," Grandpa George said.

"Open it, my dear," Grandma Georgina said. "Please open it. You're making me jumpy."

Very slowly, Charlie's fingers began to tear open one small corner of the wrapping paper.

The old people in the bed all leaned forward, craning their scraggy necks.

Then suddenly, as though he couldn't bear the suspense any longer, Charlie tore the wrapper right down the middle . . . and on to his lap, there fell . . . a light-brown creamy-colored bar of chocolate.

There was no sign of a Golden Ticket anywhere.

"Well–that's *that*!" said Grandpa Joe brightly. "It's just what we expected."

Charlie looked up. Four kind old faces were watching him intently from the bed. He smiled at them, a small sad smile, and then he shrugged his shoulders and picked up the chocolate bar and held it out to his mother, and said, "Here, Mother, have a bit. We'll share it. I want everybody to taste it."

"Certainly not!" his mother said.

And the others all cried, "No, no! We wouldn't dream of it! It's *all* yours!"

"*Please*," begged Charlie, turning round and offering it to Grandpa Joe.

But neither he nor anyone else would take even a tiny bit.

"It's time to go to school, my darling," Mrs. Bucket said, putting an arm around Charlie's skinny shoulders. "Come on, or you'll be late."

CHAPTER EIGHT

Two More Golden Tickets Found

That evening, Mr. Bucket's newspaper announced the finding of not only the third Golden Ticket, but the fourth as well. **TWO GOLDEN TICKETS FOUND TODAY**, screamed the headlines. **ONLY ONE MORE LEFT**.

"All right," said Grandpa Joe, when the whole family was gathered in the old people's room after supper, "let's hear who found them."

"The third ticket," read Mr. Bucket, holding the newspaper up close to his face because his eyes were bad and he couldn't afford glasses, "the third ticket was found by a Miss Violet Beauregarde. There was great excitement in the Beauregarde household when our reporter arrived to interview the lucky young lady—cameras were clicking and flashbulbs were flashing and people were pushing and jostling and trying to get a bit closer to the famous girl. And the famous girl was standing on a chair in the living room waving the Golden Ticket madly at arm's length as though she were flagging a taxi. She was talking very fast and very loudly to everyone, but it was not easy to hear all that she said because she was chewing so ferociously upon a piece of gum at the same time.

" 'I'm a gum chewer, normally,' she shouted, 'but when I heard about these ticket things of Mr. Wonka's, I gave up gum and started on chocolate bars in the hope of striking lucky. *Now*, of course, I'm back on gum. I just *adore* gum. I can't do without it. I munch it all day long except for a few minutes at mealtimes when I take it out and stick it behind my ear for safekeeping. To tell you the truth, I simply wouldn't feel *comfortable* if I didn't have that little wedge of gum to chew on every moment of the day, I really wouldn't. My mother says it's not ladylike and it looks ugly to see a girl's jaws going up and down like mine do all the time, but I don't agree. And who's she to criticize, anyway, because if you ask me, I'd say that *her* jaws are going up and down almost as much as mine are just from *yelling* at me every minute of the day.'

" 'Now, Violet,' Mrs. Beauregarde said from a far corner of the room where she was standing on the piano to avoid being trampled by the mob.

" 'All right, Mother, keep your hair on!' Miss Beauregarde shouted. 'And now,' she went on, turning to the reporters again, 'it may interest you to know that this piece of gum I'm chewing right at this moment is one I've been working on for over *three months solid*. That's a record, that is. It's beaten the record held by my best friend, Miss Cornelia Prinzmetel. And was she furious! It's my most treasured possession now, this piece of gum is. At nighttime, I just stick it on the end of the bedpost, and it's as good as ever in the mornings–a bit hard at first, maybe, but it soon softens up again after I've given it a few good chews. Before I started chewing for the world record, I used to change my piece of gum once a day. I used to do it in our elevator on the way home from school. Why the elevator? Because I liked sticking the gooey piece that I'd just finished with on to one of the control buttons. Then the next person who came along and pressed the button got my old gum on the end of his or her finger. Ha-ha! And what a racket they kicked up, some of them. You get the best results with women who have expensive gloves on. Oh yes, I'm thrilled to be going to Mr. Wonka's factory. And I understand that afterwards he's going to give me enough gum to last me for the rest of my whole life. Whoopee! Hooray!' "

"*Beastly* girl," said Grandma Josephine.

"Despicable!" said Grandma Georgina. "She'll come to a sticky end one day, chewing all that gum, you see if she doesn't."

"And who got the fourth Golden Ticket?" Charlie asked.

"Now, let me see," said Mr. Bucket, peering at the newspaper again. "Ah yes, here we are. The fourth Golden Ticket," he read, "was found by a boy called Mike Teavee."

"Another bad lot, I'll be bound," muttered Grandma Josephine.

"Don't interrupt, Grandma," said Mrs. Bucket.

"The Teavee household," said Mr. Bucket, going on with his reading, "was crammed, like all the others, with excited visitors when our reporter arrived, but young Mike Teavee, the lucky winner, seemed extremely annoyed by the whole business. 'Can't you fools see I'm watching television?' he said angrily. 'I wish you wouldn't interrupt!'

"The nine-year-old boy was seated before an

enormous television set, with his eyes glued to the screen, and he was watching a film in which one bunch of gangsters was shooting up another bunch of gangsters with machine guns. Mike Teavee himself had no less than eighteen toy pistols of various sizes hanging from belts around his body, and every now and again he would leap up into the air and fire off half a dozen rounds from one or another of these weapons.

" 'Quiet!' he shouted, when someone tried to ask him a question. 'Didn't I *tell* you not to interrupt! This show's an absolute whiz-banger! It's terrific! I watch it every day. I watch all of them every day, even the rotten ones, where there's no shooting. I like the gangsters best. They're terrific, those gangsters! Especially when they start pumping each other full of lead, or flashing the old stilettos, or giving each other the one-two-three with their knuckledusters! Gosh, what wouldn't I give to be doing that myself! It's the *life*, I tell you! It's terrific!' "

"That's quite enough!" snapped Grandma Josephine. "I can't *bear* to listen to it!"

"Nor me," said Grandma Georgina. "Do *all* children behave like this nowadays–like these brats we've been hearing about?"

"Of course not," said Mr. Bucket, smiling at the old lady in the bed. "Some do, of course. In fact, quite a lot of them do. But not *all*."

"And now there's only *one ticket left!*" said Grandpa George.

"Quite so," sniffed Grandma Georgina. "And just as sure as I'll be having cabbage soup for supper tomorrow, that ticket'll go to some nasty little beast who doesn't deserve it!"

CHAPTER NINE

Grandpa Joe Takes a Gamble

The next day, when Charlie came home from school and went in to see his grandparents, he found that only Grandpa Joe was awake. The other three were all snoring loudly.

"Ssshh!" whispered Grandpa Joe, and he beckoned Charlie to come closer. Charlie tiptoed over and stood beside the bed. The old man gave Charlie a sly grin, and then he started rummaging under his pillow with one hand; and when the hand came out again, there was an ancient leather purse clutched in the fingers. Under cover of the bedclothes, the old man opened the purse and tipped it upside down. Out fell a single silver sixpence. "It's my secret hoard," he whispered. "The others don't know I've got it. And now, you and I are going to have one more fling at finding that last ticket. How about it, eh? But you'll have to help me."

"Are you *sure* you want to spend your money on that, Grandpa?" Charlie whispered.

"Of course I'm sure!" spluttered the old man excitedly. "Don't stand there arguing! I'm as keen as you are to find that ticket! Here—take the money and run down the street to the nearest shop and buy the first Wonka bar you see and bring it straight back to me, and we'll open it together."

Charlie took the little silver coin, and slipped quickly out of the room. In five minutes, he was back.

"Have you got it?" whispered Grandpa Joe, his eyes shining with excitement.

Charlie nodded and held out the bar of chocolate. WONKA'S NUTTY CRUNCH SURPRISE, it said on the wrapper.

"Good!" the old man whispered, sitting up in the bed and rubbing his hands. "Now—come over here and sit close to me and we'll open it together. Are you ready?"

"Yes," Charlie said. "I'm ready."

"All right. You tear off the first bit."

"No," Charlie said, "you paid for it. You do it all."

The old man's fingers were trembling most terribly as they fumbled with the wrapper. "We don't have a hope, really," he whispered, giggling a bit. "You do know we don't have a hope, don't you?"

"Yes," Charlie said. "I know that."

They looked at each other, and both started giggling nervously.

"Mind you," said Grandpa Joe, "there is just that *tiny* chance that it *might* be the one, don't you agree?"

"Yes," Charlie said. "Of course. Why don't you open it, Grandpa?"

"All in good time, my boy, all in good time. Which end do you think I ought to open first?"

"That corner. The one furthest from you. Just tear off a *tiny* bit, but not quite enough for us to see anything."

"Like that?" said the old man.

"Yes. Now a little bit more."

"You finish it," said Grandpa Joe. "I'm too nervous."

"No, Grandpa. You must do it yourself."

"Very well, then. Here goes." He tore off the wrapper.

They both stared at what lay underneath. It was a bar of chocolate—nothing more.

All at once, they both saw the funny side of the whole thing, and they burst into peals of laughter.

"What on earth's going on!" cried Grandma Josephine, waking up suddenly.

"Nothing," said Grandpa Joe. "You go on back to sleep."

CHAPTER TEN

The Family Begins to Starve

During the next two weeks, the weather turned very cold. First came the snow. It began very suddenly one morning just as Charlie Bucket was getting dressed for school. Standing by the window, he saw the huge flakes drifting slowly down out of an icy sky that was the color of steel.

By evening, it lay four feet deep around the tiny house, and Mr. Bucket had to dig a path from the front door to the road.

After the snow, there came a freezing gale that blew for days and days without stopping. And oh, how bitter cold it was! Everything that Charlie touched seemed to be made of ice, and each time he stepped outside the door, the wind was like a knife on his cheek.

Inside the house, little jets of freezing air came rushing in through the sides of the windows and under the doors, and there was no place to go to escape them. The four old ones lay silent and huddled in their bed, trying to keep the cold out of their bones. The excitement over the Golden Tickets had long since been forgotten. Nobody in the family gave a thought now to anything except the two vital problems of trying to keep warm and trying to get enough to eat.

There is something about very cold weather that gives one an enormous appetite. Most of us find ourselves beginning to crave rich steaming stews and hot apple pies and all kinds of delicious warming dishes; and because we are all a great deal luckier than we realize, we usually get what we want—or near enough. But Charlie Bucket never got what he wanted because the family couldn't afford it, and as the cold weather went on and on, he became ravenously and desperately hungry. Both bars of chocolate, the birthday one and the one Grandpa Joe had bought, had long since been nibbled away, and all he got now were those thin, cabbagy meals three times a day.

Then all at once, the meals became even thinner.

The reason for this was that the toothpaste factory, the place where Mr. Bucket worked, suddenly went bust and had to close down. Quickly, Mr. Bucket tried to get another job. But he had no luck. In the end, the only way in which he managed to earn a few pennies was by shoveling snow in the streets. But it wasn't enough to buy even a quarter of the food that seven people needed. The situation became desperate. Breakfast was a single slice of bread for each person now, and lunch was maybe half a boiled potato.

Slowly but surely, everybody in the house began to starve.

And every day, little Charlie Bucket, trudging through the snow on his way to school, would have to pass Mr. Willy Wonka's giant chocolate factory. And every day, as he came near to it, he would lift his small pointed nose high in the air and sniff the wonderful sweet smell of melting chocolate. Sometimes, he would stand motionless outside the gates for several minutes on end, taking deep swallowing breaths as though he were trying to *eat* the smell itself.

"That child," said Grandpa Joe, poking his head up from under the blanket one icy morning, "that child has *got* to have more food. It doesn't matter about us. We're too old to bother with. But a *growing boy*! He can't go on like this! He's beginning to look like a skeleton!"

"What can one *do*?" murmured Grandma Josephine miserably. "He refuses to take any of ours. I hear his mother tried to slip her own piece of bread on to his plate at breakfast this morning, but he wouldn't touch it. He made her take it back."

Charlie and the Chocolate Factory

The Family Begins to Starve

"He's a fine little fellow," said Grandpa George. "He deserves better than this."

The cruel weather went on and on.

And every day, Charlie Bucket grew thinner and thinner. His face became frighteningly white and pinched. The skin was drawn so tightly over the cheeks that you could see the shapes of the bones underneath. It seemed doubtful whether he could go on much longer like this without becoming dangerously ill.

And now, very calmly, with that curious wisdom that seems to come so often to small children in times of hardship, he began to make little changes here and there in some of the things that he did, so as to save his strength. In the mornings, he left the house ten minutes earlier so that he could walk slowly to school, without ever having to run. He sat quietly in the classroom during break, resting himself, while the others rushed outdoors and threw snowballs and wrestled in the snow. Everything he did now, he did slowly and carefully, to prevent exhaustion.

Then one afternoon, walking back home with the icy wind in his face (and incidentally feeling hungrier than he had ever felt before), his eye was caught suddenly by something silvery lying in the gutter, in the snow. Charlie stepped off the curb and bent down to examine it. Part of it was buried under the snow, but he saw at once what it was.

It was a fifty-pence piece!

Quickly he looked around him.

Had somebody just dropped it?

No–that was impossible because of the way part of it was buried.

Several people went hurrying past him on the pavement, their chins sunk deep in the collars of their coats, their feet crunching in the snow. None of them was searching for any money; none of them was taking the slightest notice of the small boy crouching in the gutter.

Then was it *his*, this fifty pence?

Could he *have* it?

Carefully, Charlie pulled it out from under the snow. It was damp and dirty, but otherwise perfect.

A WHOLE fifty pence!

He held it tightly between his shivering fingers, gazing down at it. It meant one thing to him at that moment, only *one* thing. It meant FOOD.

Automatically, Charlie turned and began moving toward the nearest shop. It was only ten paces away . . . it was a newspaper and stationery shop, the kind that sells almost everything, including sweets and cigars . . . and what he would *do*, he whispered quickly to himself . . . he would buy one luscious bar of chocolate and eat it *all* up, every bit of it, right then and there . . . and the rest of the money he would take straight back home and give to his mother.

CHAPTER ELEVEN

The Miracle

Charlie entered the shop and laid the fifty-pence piece on the counter.

"One Wonka's Whipple-Scrumptious Fudgemallow Delight," he said, remembering how much he had loved the one he had on his birthday.

The man behind the counter looked fat and well-fed. He had big lips and fat cheeks and a very fat neck. The fat around his neck bulged out all around the top of his collar like a rubber ring. He turned and reached behind him for the chocolate bar, then he turned back again and handed it to Charlie. Charlie grabbed it and quickly tore off the wrapper and took an enormous bite. Then he took another . . . and another . . . and oh, the joy of being able to cram large pieces of something sweet and solid into one's mouth! The sheer blissful joy of being able to fill one's mouth with rich solid food!

"You look like you wanted that one, sonny," the shopkeeper said pleasantly.

Charlie nodded, his mouth bulging with chocolate.

The shopkeeper put Charlie's change on the counter. "Take it easy," he said. "It'll give you a tummy ache if you swallow it like that without chewing."

Charlie went on wolfing the chocolate. He couldn't stop. And in less than half a minute, the whole thing had disappeared down his throat. He was quite out of breath, but he felt marvelously, extraordinarily happy. He reached out a hand to take the change. Then he paused. His eyes were just above the level of the counter. They were staring at the

silver coins lying there. The coins were all five-penny pieces. There were nine of them altogether. Surely it wouldn't matter if he spent just one more . . .

"I think," he said quietly, "I think . . . I'll have just one more of those chocolate bars. The same kind as before, please."

"Why not?" the fat shopkeeper said, reaching behind him again and taking another Whipple-Scrumptious Fudgemallow Delight from the shelf. He laid it on the counter.

Charlie picked it up and tore off the wrapper . . . and *suddenly* . . . from underneath the wrapper . . . there came a brilliant flash of gold.

Charlie's heart stood still.

"It's a Golden Ticket!" screamed the shopkeeper, leaping about a foot in the air. "You've got a Golden Ticket! You've found the last Golden Ticket! Hey, would you believe it! Come and look at this, everybody! The kid's found Wonka's last Golden Ticket! There it is! It's right here in his hands!"

The Miracle

It seemed as though the shopkeeper might be going to have a fit. "In my shop, too!" he yelled. "He found it right here in my own little shop! Somebody call the newspapers quick and let them know! Watch out now, sonny! Don't tear it as you unwrap it! That thing's precious!"

In a few seconds, there was a crowd of about twenty people clustering around Charlie, and many more were pushing their way in from the street. Everybody wanted to get a look at the Golden Ticket and at the lucky finder.

"Where is it?" somebody shouted. "Hold it up so all of us can see it!"

"There it is, there!" someone else shouted. "He's holding it in his hands! See the gold shining!"

"How did *he* manage to find it, I'd like to know?" a large boy shouted angrily. "*Twenty* bars a day I've been buying for weeks and weeks!"

"Think of all the free stuff he'll be getting too!" another boy said enviously. "A lifetime supply!"

"He'll need it, the skinny little shrimp!" a girl said, laughing.

Charlie hadn't moved. He hadn't even unwrapped the Golden Ticket from around the chocolate. He was standing very still, holding it tightly with both hands while the crowd pushed and shouted all around him. He felt quite dizzy. There was a peculiar floating sensation coming over him, as though he were floating up in the air like a balloon. His feet didn't seem to be touching the ground at all. He could hear his heart thumping away loudly somewhere in his throat.

At that point, he became aware of a hand resting lightly on his shoulder, and when he looked up, he saw a tall man standing over him. "Listen," the man whispered. "I'll buy it from you. I'll give you fifty pounds. How about it, eh? And I'll give you a new bicycle as well. Okay?"

"Are you *crazy*?" shouted a woman who was standing equally close. "Why, I'd give him *two hundred* pounds for that ticket! You want to sell that ticket for two hundred pounds, young man?"

"That's *quite* enough of that!" the fat shopkeeper shouted, pushing his way through the crowd and taking Charlie firmly by the arm. "Leave the kid alone, will you! Make way there! Let him out!" And to Charlie, as he led him to the door, he whispered, "Don't you let *anybody* have it! Take it straight home, quickly, before you lose it! Run all the way and don't stop till you get there, you understand?"

Charlie nodded.

"You know something," the fat shopkeeper said, pausing a moment and smiling at Charlie, "I have a feeling you needed a break like this. I'm awfully glad you got it. Good luck to you, sonny."

"Thank you," Charlie said, and off he went, running through the snow as fast as his legs would go. And as he flew past Mr. Willy Wonka's factory, he turned and waved at it and sang out, "I'll be seeing you! I'll be seeing you soon!" And five minutes later he arrived at his own home.

CHAPTER TWELVE

What It Said on the Golden Ticket

Charlie burst through the front door, shouting, "*Mother! Mother! Mother!*"

Mrs. Bucket was in the old grandparents' room, serving them their evening soup.

"*Mother!*" yelled Charlie, rushing in on them like a hurricane. "Look! I've got it! Look, Mother, look! The last Golden Ticket! It's mine! I found some money in the street and I bought two bars of chocolate and the second one had the Golden Ticket and there were *crowds* of people all around me wanting to see it and the shopkeeper rescued me and I ran all the way home and here I am! IT'S THE FIFTH GOLDEN TICKET, MOTHER, AND I'VE FOUND IT!"

Mrs. Bucket simply stood and stared, while the four old grandparents, who were sitting up in bed balancing bowls of soup on their laps, all dropped their spoons with a clatter and froze against their pillows.

For about ten seconds there was absolute silence in the room. Nobody dared to speak or move. It was a magic moment.

Then, very softly, Grandpa Joe said, "You're pulling our legs, Charlie, aren't you? You're having a little joke?"

"I am *not*!" cried Charlie, rushing up to the bed and holding out the large and beautiful Golden Ticket for him to see.

Grandpa Joe leaned forward and took a close look, his nose almost

45

touching the ticket. The others watched him, waiting for the verdict.

Then very slowly, with a slow and marvelous grin spreading all over his face, Grandpa Joe lifted his head and looked straight at Charlie. The color was rushing to his cheeks, and his eyes were wide open, shining with joy, and in the center of each eye, right in the very center, in the black pupil, a little spark of wild excitement was slowly dancing. Then the old man took a deep breath, and suddenly, with no warning whatsoever, an explosion seemed to take place inside him. He threw up his arms and yelled "*Yippeeeeeeee!*" And at the same time, his long bony body rose up out of the bed and his bowl of soup went flying into the face of Grandma Josephine, and in one fantastic leap, this old fellow of ninety-six and a half, who hadn't been out

of bed these last twenty years, jumped on to the floor and started doing a dance of victory in his pajamas.

"Yippeeeeeeeeee!" he shouted. "Three cheers for Charlie! Hip, hip, hooray!"

At this point, the door opened, and Mr. Bucket walked into the room. He was cold and tired, and he looked it. All day long, he had been shoveling snow in the streets.

"*Cripes!*" he cried. "What's going on in here?"

It didn't take them long to tell him what had happened.

"I don't believe it!" he said. "It's not possible."

"Show him the ticket, Charlie!" shouted Grandpa Joe, who was still dancing around the floor like a dervish in his striped pajamas. "Show your father the fifth and last Golden Ticket in the world!"

"Let me see it, Charlie," Mr. Bucket said, collapsing into a chair and holding out his hand. Charlie came forward with the precious document.

It was a very beautiful thing, this Golden Ticket, having been made, so it seemed, from a sheet of pure gold hammered out almost to the thinness of paper. On one side of it, printed by some clever method in jet-black letters, was the invitation itself–from Mr. Wonka.

"Read it aloud," said Grandpa Joe, climbing back into bed again at last. "Let's all hear exactly what it says."

Mr. Bucket held the lovely Golden Ticket up close to his eyes. His hands were trembling slightly, and he seemed to be overcome by the whole business. He took several deep breaths. Then he cleared his throat, and said, "All right, I'll read it. Here we go:

"*Greetings to you*, the lucky finder of this Golden Ticket, from Mr. Willy Wonka! I shake you warmly by the hand! Tremendous things are in store for you! Many wonderful surprises await you! For now, I do invite you to come to my factory and be my guest for one whole day–you and all others who are lucky enough to find my Golden Tickets. I, Willy Wonka, will conduct you around the factory myself, showing you everything that there is to see, and afterwards, when it is time to leave, you will be escorted home by a procession of large trucks. These trucks, I can promise you, will be loaded with enough delicious eatables to last you and your entire household for many years. If, at any time thereafter, you should run out of supplies, you have only to come back to the factory and show this Golden Ticket, and I shall be happy to refill your cupboard with whatever you want. In this way, you will be able to keep yourself supplied with tasty morsels for the rest of your life. But this is by no means the most exciting thing that will happen on the day of your visit. I am preparing other surprises that are even more marvelous and more fantastic for you and for all my beloved Golden Ticket holders–mystic and marvelous surprises that will entrance, delight, intrigue, astonish, and perplex you beyond measure. In your wildest dreams you could not imagine that such things could happen to you! Just wait and see! And now, here are your instructions: the day I have chosen for the visit is the first day in the month of February. On this day, and on no other, you must come to the factory gates at ten o'clock sharp in the morning. Don't be late! And you are allowed to bring with you either one or two members of your own family to look after you and to ensure that you don't get into mischief. One more thing–be certain to have this ticket with you, otherwise you will not be admitted.

(Signed) **Willy Wonka**."

What It Said on the Golden Ticket

"The first day of *February*!" cried Mrs. Bucket. "But that's *tomorrow*! Today is the last day of January. *I know it is!*"

"Cripes!" said Mr. Bucket. "I think you're right!"

"You're just in time!" shouted Grandpa Joe. "There's not a moment to lose. You must start making preparations at once! Wash your face, comb your hair, scrub your hands, brush your teeth, blow your nose, cut your nails, polish your shoes, iron your shirt, and for heaven's sake, get all that mud off your pants! You must get ready, my boy! You must get ready for the biggest day of your life!"

"Now don't over-excite yourself, Grandpa," Mrs. Bucket said. "And don't fluster poor Charlie. We must all try to keep very calm. Now the first thing to decide is this—who is going to go with Charlie to the factory?"

"I will!" shouted Grandpa Joe, leaping out of bed once again. "I'll take him! I'll look after him! You leave it to me!"

Mrs. Bucket smiled at the old man, then she turned to her husband and said, "How about you, dear? Don't you think *you* ought to go?"

"Well . . ." Mr. Bucket said, pausing to think about it, "no . . . I'm not so sure that I should."

"But you *must.*"

"There's no *must* about it, my dear," Mr. Bucket said gently. "Mind you, I'd *love* to go. It'll be tremendously exciting. But on the other hand . . . I believe that the person who really *deserves* to go most of all is Grandpa Joe himself. He seems to know more about it than we do. Provided, of course, that he feels well enough . . ."

"Yippeeeeee!" shouted Grandpa Joe, seizing Charlie by the hands and dancing round the room.

"He certainly *seems* well enough," Mrs. Bucket said, laughing. "Yes . . . perhaps you're right after all. Perhaps Grandpa Joe should be the one to go with him. I certainly can't go myself and leave the other three old people all alone in bed for a whole day."

"Hallelujah!" yelled Grandpa Joe. "Praise the Lord!"

At that point, there came a loud knock on the front door. Mr. Bucket went to open it, and the next moment, swarms of newspapermen and photographers were pouring into the house. They had tracked down the finder of the fifth Golden Ticket, and now they all wanted to get the full story for the front pages of the morning papers. For several hours, there was complete pandemonium in the little house, and it must have been nearly midnight before Mr. Bucket was able to get rid of them so that Charlie could go to bed.

CHAPTER THIRTEEN
The Big Day Arrives

The sun was shining brightly on the morning of the big day, but the ground was still white with snow and the air was very cold.

Outside the gates of Wonka's factory, enormous crowds of people had gathered to watch the five lucky ticket holders going in. The excitement was tremendous. It was just before ten o'clock. The crowds were pushing and shouting, and policemen with arms linked were trying to hold them back from the gates.

Right beside the gates, in a small group that was carefully shielded from the crowds by the police, stood the five famous children, together with the grown-ups who had come with them.

The tall bony figure of Grandpa Joe could be seen standing quietly among them, and beside him, holding tightly on to his hand, was little Charlie Bucket himself.

All the children, except Charlie, had both their mothers and fathers with them, and it was a good thing that they had, otherwise the whole party might have got out of hand. They were so eager to get going that their parents were having to hold them back by force to prevent them from climbing over the gates. "Be patient!" cried the fathers. "Be still! It's not *time* yet! It's not ten o'clock!"

Behind him, Charlie Bucket could hear the shouts of the people in the crowd as they pushed and fought to get a glimpse of the famous children.

"There's Violet Beauregarde!" he heard someone shouting. "That's her all right! I can remember her face from the newspapers!"

"And you know what?" somebody else shouted back. "She's still chewing that dreadful old piece of gum she's had for three months! You look at her jaws! They're still working on it!"

"Who's the big fat boy?"

"That's Augustus Gloop!"

"So it is!"

"Enormous, isn't he!"

"Fantastic!"

"Who's the kid with a picture of The Lone Ranger stenciled on his Windbreaker?"

"That's Mike Teavee! He's the television fiend!"

"He must be crazy! Look at all those toy pistols he's got hanging all over him!"

"The one I want to see is Veruca Salt!" shouted another voice in the crowd. "She's the girl whose father bought up half a million chocolate bars and then made the workers in his peanut factory unwrap every one of them until they found a Golden Ticket! He gives her anything

she wants! Absolutely anything! She only has to start screaming for it and she gets it!"

"Dreadful, isn't it?"

"Shocking, I call it!"

"Which do you think is her?"

"That one! Over there on the left! The little girl in the silver mink coat!"

"Which one is Charlie Bucket?"

"Charlie Bucket? He must be that skinny little shrimp standing beside the old fellow who looks like a skeleton. Very close to us. Just there! See him?"

"Why hasn't he got a coat on in this cold weather?"

"Don't ask me. Maybe he can't afford to buy one."

"Goodness me! He must be freezing!"

Charlie, standing only a few paces away from the speaker, gave Grandpa Joe's hand a squeeze, and the old man looked down at Charlie and smiled.

Somewhere in the distance, a church clock began striking ten.

Very slowly, with a loud creaking of rusty hinges, the great iron gates of the factory began to swing open.

The crowd became suddenly silent. The children stopped jumping about. All eyes were fixed upon the gates.

"*There he is!*" somebody shouted. "*That's him!*"

And so it was!

CHAPTER FOURTEEN

Mr. Willy Wonka

Mr. Wonka was standing all alone just inside the open gates of the factory.

And what an extraordinary little man he was!

He had a black top hat on his head.

He wore a tail coat made of a beautiful plum-colored velvet.

His trousers were bottle green.

His gloves were pearly gray.

And in one hand he carried a fine gold-topped walking cane.

Covering his chin, there was a small, neat, pointed black beard–a goatee. And his eyes–his eyes were most marvelously bright. They seemed to be sparkling and twinkling at you all the time. The whole face, in fact, was alight with fun and laughter.

And oh, how clever he looked! How quick and sharp and full of life! He kept making quick jerky little movements with his head, cocking it this way and that, and taking everything in with those bright twinkling eyes. He was like a squirrel in the quickness of his movements, like a quick clever old squirrel from the park.

Suddenly, he did a funny little skipping dance in the snow, and he spread his arms wide, and he smiled at the five children who were clustered near the gates, and he called out, "Welcome, my little friends! Welcome to the factory!"

His voice was high and flutey. "Will you come forward one at a time, please," he called out, "and bring your parents. Then show me your Golden Ticket and give me your name. Who's first?"

The big fat boy stepped up. "I'm Augustus Gloop," he said.

"Augustus!" cried Mr. Wonka, seizing his hand and pumping it up and down with terrific force. "My *dear* boy, how *good* to see you! Delighted! Charmed! Overjoyed to have you with us! And *these* are your parents? How *nice!* Come in! Come in! That's right! Step through the gates!"

Mr. Wonka was clearly just as excited as everybody else.

"My name," said the next child to go forward, "is Veruca Salt."

"My *dear* Veruca! How *do* you do? What a pleasure this is! You *do* have an interesting name, don't you? I always thought that a verruca was a sort of wart that you got on the sole of your foot! But I must be wrong, mustn't I? How pretty you look in that lovely mink coat! I'm so glad you could come! Dear me, this is going to be *such* an exciting day! I *do* hope you enjoy it! I'm sure you *will*! I *know* you will! Your father? How *are* you, Mr. Salt? And Mrs. Salt? Overjoyed to see you! Yes, the ticket is *quite* in order! Please go in!"

Mr. Willy Wonka

The next two children, Violet Beauregarde and Mike Teavee, came forward to have their tickets examined and then to have their arms practically pumped off their shoulders by the energetic Mr. Wonka.

And last of all, a small nervous voice whispered, "Charlie Bucket."

"Charlie!" cried Mr. Wonka. "Well, well, well! So *there* you are! You're the one who found your ticket only yesterday, aren't you? Yes, yes. I read *all* about it in this morning's papers! *Just* in time, my dear boy! I'm so glad! So happy for you! And this? Your grandfather? Delighted to meet you, sir! Overjoyed! Enraptured! Enchanted! All right! Excellent! Is everybody in now? Five children? Yes! Good! Now will you please follow me! Our tour is about to begin! But *do* keep together! *Please* don't wander off by yourselves! I shouldn't like to lose any of you at *this* stage of the proceedings! Oh, dear me, no!"

Charlie glanced back over his shoulder and saw the great iron entrance gates slowly closing behind him. The crowds on the outside were still pushing and shouting. Charlie took a last look at them. Then, as the gates closed with a clang, all sight of the outside world disappeared.

"Here we are!" cried Mr. Wonka, trotting along in front of the group. "Through this big red door, please! *That's* right! It's nice and warm inside! I have to keep it warm inside the factory because of the workers! My workers are used to an *extremely* hot climate! They can't stand the cold! They'd perish if they went outdoors in this weather! They'd freeze to death!"

"But who *are* these workers?" asked Augustus Gloop.

"All in good time, my dear boy!" said Mr. Wonka, smiling at Augustus. "Be patient! You shall see everything as we go along! Are all of you inside? Good! Would you mind closing the door? Thank you!"

Charlie Bucket found himself standing in a long corridor that stretched away in front of him as far as he could see. The corridor was so wide that a car could easily have been driven along it. The walls were pale pink, the lighting was soft and pleasant.

"How lovely and warm!" whispered Charlie.

"I know. And what a marvelous smell!" answered Grandpa Joe, taking a long deep sniff. All the most wonderful smells in the world seemed to be mixed up in the air around them—the smell of roasting coffee and burnt sugar and melting chocolate and mint and violets and crushed hazelnuts and apple blossom and caramel and lemon peel . . .

And far away in the distance, from the heart of the great factory, came a muffled roar of energy as though some monstrous gigantic machine were spinning its wheels at breakneck speed.

"Now *this*, my dear children," said Mr. Wonka, raising his voice above the noise, "this is the main corridor. Will you please hang your coats and hats on those pegs over there, and then follow me. *That's* the way! Good! Everyone ready? Come on, then! Here we go!" He trotted off rapidly down the corridor with the tails of his plum-colored velvet coat flapping behind him, and the visitors all hurried after him.

It was quite a large party of people, when you came to think of it. There were nine grown-ups and five children, fourteen in all. So you can imagine that there was a good deal of pushing and shoving as they hustled and bustled down the passage, trying to keep up with the swift little figure in front of them. "Come *on*!" cried Mr. Wonka. "Get a move on, please! We'll *never* get round today if you dawdle like this!"

Soon, he turned right off the main corridor into another slightly
narrower passage.

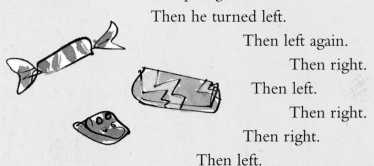

Then he turned left.

Then left again.

Then right.

Then left.

Then right.

Then right.

Then left.

The place was like a gigantic rabbit warren, with passages leading this way and that in every direction.

"Don't you let go my hand, Charlie," whispered Grandpa Joe.

"Notice how all these passages are sloping downward!" called out Mr. Wonka. "We are now going underground! *All* the most important rooms in my factory are deep down below the surface!"

"Why is that?" somebody asked.

"There wouldn't be *nearly* enough space for them up on top!" answered Mr. Wonka. "These rooms we are going to see are *enormous*! They're larger than football fields! No building in the *world* would be big enough to house them! But down here, underneath the ground, I've got *all* the space I want. There's no limit—so long as I hollow it out."

Mr. Wonka turned right.

He turned left.

He turned right again.

The passages were sloping steeper and steeper downhill now.

Then suddenly, Mr. Wonka stopped. In front of him, there was a shiny metal door. The party crowded round. On the door, in large letters, it said:

THE CHOCOLATE ROOM

CHAPTER FIFTEEN
The Chocolate Room

"An important room, this!" cried Mr. Wonka, taking a bunch of keys from his pocket and slipping one into the keyhole of the door. "*This* is the nerve center of the whole factory, the heart of the whole business! And so *beautiful*! I *insist* upon my rooms being beautiful! I can't *abide* ugliness in factories! *In* we go, then! But *do* be careful, my dear children! Don't lose your heads! Don't get overexcited! Keep very calm!"

Mr. Wonka opened the door. Five children and nine grown-ups pushed their ways in—and *oh*, what an amazing sight it was that now met their eyes!

They were looking down upon a lovely valley. There were green meadows on either side of the valley, and along the bottom of it there flowed a great brown river.

What is more, there was a tremendous waterfall halfway along the river—a steep cliff over which the water curled and rolled in a solid sheet, and then went crashing down into a boiling churning whirlpool of froth and spray.

Below the waterfall (and this was the most astonishing sight of all), a whole mass of enormous glass pipes were dangling down into the river from somewhere high up in the ceiling! They really were *enormous*, those pipes. There must have been a dozen of them at least, and they were sucking up the brownish muddy water from the river and carrying it away to goodness knows where. And because they were made of glass, you could see the liquid flowing and bubbling along inside them, and

The Chocolate Room

above the noise of the waterfall, you could hear the never-ending suck-suck-sucking sound of the pipes as they did their work.

Graceful trees and bushes were growing along the riverbanks—weeping willows and alders and tall clumps of rhododendrons with their pink and red and mauve blossoms. In the meadows there were thousands of buttercups.

"*There!*" cried Mr. Wonka, dancing up and down and pointing his gold-topped cane at the great brown river. "It's *all* chocolate! Every drop of that river is hot melted chocolate of the finest quality. The *very* finest quality. There's enough chocolate in there to fill *every* bathtub in the *entire* country! *And* all the swimming pools as well! Isn't it *terrific*? And just look at my pipes! They suck up the chocolate and carry it away to all the other rooms in the factory where it is needed! Thousands of gallons an hour, my dear children! Thousands and thousands of gallons!"

The children and their parents were too flabbergasted to speak. They were staggered. They were dumbfounded. They were bewildered and dazzled. They were completely bowled over by the hugeness of the whole thing. They simply stood and stared.

"The waterfall is *most* important!" Mr. Wonka went on. "It mixes the chocolate! It churns it up! It pounds it and beats it! It makes it light and frothy! No other factory in the world mixes its chocolate by waterfall! But it's the *only* way to do it properly! The *only* way! And do you like my trees?" he cried, pointing with his stick. "And my lovely bushes? Don't you think they look pretty? I told you I hated ugliness! And of course they are *all* eatable! All made of something different and delicious! And do you like my meadows? Do you like my grass and my buttercups? The grass you are standing on, my dear little ones, is made of a new kind of soft, minty sugar that I've just invented! I call it swudge! Try a blade! Please do! It's delectable!"

Automatically, everybody bent down and picked one blade of grass—everybody, that is, except Augustus Gloop, who took a big handful.

And Violet Beauregarde, before tasting her blade of grass, took the piece of world-record-breaking chewing-gum out of her mouth and stuck it carefully behind her ear.

"Isn't it *wonderful*!" whispered Charlie. "Hasn't it got a wonderful taste, Grandpa?"

"I could eat the whole *field*!" said Grandpa Joe, grinning with delight. "I could go around on all fours like a cow and eat every blade of grass in the field!"

"Try a buttercup!" cried Mr. Wonka. "They're even *nicer*!"

Suddenly, the air was filled with screams of excitement. The screams came from Veruca Salt. She was pointing frantically to the other side of the river. "*Look!* Look over there!" she screamed. "What *is* it? He's moving! He's walking! It's a little *person*! It's a little *man*! Down there below the waterfall!"

Everybody stopped picking buttercups and stared across the river.

"*She's right, Grandpa!*" cried Charlie. "It *is* a little man! Can you *see* him?"

"I see him, Charlie!" said Grandpa Joe excitedly.

And now everybody started shouting at once.

"There's *two* of them!"

"My gosh, so there is!"

"There's more than two! There's one, two, three, four, five!"

"What are they *doing*?"

"Where do they *come* from?"

"Who *are* they?"

Children and parents alike rushed down to the edge of the river to get a closer look.

"Aren't they *fantastic*!"

"No higher than my knee!"

"Look at their funny long hair!"

The tiny men–they were no larger than medium-sized dolls–had stopped what they were doing, and now they were staring back across the river at the visitors. One of them pointed toward the children, and then he whispered something to the other four, and all five of them burst into peals of laughter.

"But they can't be *real* people," Charlie said.

"Of course they're real people," Mr. Wonka answered. "They're Oompa-Loompas."

CHAPTER SIXTEEN

The Oompa-Loompas

"*O*ompa-Loompas!" everyone said at once. "*Oompa-Loompas!*"

"Imported direct from Loompaland," said Mr. Wonka proudly.

"There's no such place," said Mrs. Salt.

"Excuse me, dear lady, but . . ."

"*Mr. Wonka,*" cried Mrs. Salt. "I'm a teacher of geography . . ."

"Then you'll know all about it," said Mr. Wonka. "And oh, what a terrible country it is! Nothing but thick jungles infested by the most dangerous beasts in the world–hornswogglers and snozzwangers and those terrible wicked whangdoodles. A whangdoodle would eat ten Oompa-Loompas for breakfast and come galloping back for a second helping. When I went out there, I found the little Oompa-Loompas living in tree houses. They *had* to live in tree houses to escape from the whangdoodles and the hornswogglers and the snozzwangers. And they were living on green caterpillars, and the caterpillars tasted revolting, and the Oompa-Loompas spent every moment of their days climbing through the treetops looking for other things to mash up with the caterpillars to make them taste better– red beetles, for instance, and eucalyptus leaves, and the bark of the bong-bong tree, all of them beastly, but not quite so beastly as the caterpillars. Poor little Oompa-Loompas! The one food that they longed for more than any other was the cacao bean. But they couldn't get it. An Oompa-Loompa was lucky if he

found three or four cacao beans a year. But oh, how they craved them. They used to dream about cacao beans all night and talk about them all day. You had only to *mention* the word 'cacao' to an Oompa-Loompa and he would start dribbling at the mouth. The cacao bean," Mr. Wonka continued, "which grows on the cacao tree, happens to be *the thing* from which all chocolate is made. You cannot make chocolate without the cacao bean. The cacao bean *is* chocolate. I myself use billions of cacao beans every week in this factory. And so, my dear children, as soon as I discovered that the Oompa-Loompas were crazy about this particular food, I climbed up to their tree-house village and poked my head in through the door of the tree house belonging to the leader of the tribe. The poor little fellow, looking thin and starved, was sitting there trying to eat a bowl full of mashed-up green caterpillars without being sick. 'Look here,' I said (speaking not in English, of course, but in Oompa-Loompish), 'look here, if you and all your people will come back to my country and live in my factory, you can have *all* the cacao beans you want! I've got mountains of them in my storehouses! You can have cacao beans for every meal! You can gorge yourselves silly on them! I'll even pay your wages in cacao beans if you wish!"

" 'You really mean it?' asked the Oompa-Loompa leader, leaping up from his chair.

" 'Of course I mean it,' I said. 'And you can have chocolate as well. Chocolate tastes even better than cacao beans because it's got milk and sugar added.'

"The little man gave a great whoop of joy and threw his bowl of mashed caterpillars right out of the tree-house window. 'It's a deal!' he cried. 'Come on! Let's go!'

"So I shipped them all over here, every man, woman, and child in the Oompa-Loompa tribe. It was easy. I smuggled them over in large packing cases with holes in them, and they all got here safely. They are wonderful workers. They all speak English now. They love dancing and music. They are always making up songs. I expect you will hear a good deal of singing today from time to time. I must warn you, though, that they are rather mischievous. They like jokes. They still wear the same kind of clothes they wore in the jungle. They insist upon that. The men, as you can see for yourselves across the river, wear only deerskins. The women wear leaves, and the children wear nothing at all. The women use fresh leaves every day . . ."

"*Daddy!*" shouted Veruca Salt (the girl who got everything she wanted). "*Daddy!* I want an Oompa-Loompa! I want you to get me an Oompa-Loompa! I want an Oompa-Loompa right away! I want to take it home with me! Go on, Daddy! Get me an Oompa-Loompa!"

"Now, now, my pet!" her father said to her, "we mustn't interrupt Mr. Wonka."

"*But I want an Oompa-Loompa!*" screamed Veruca.

"All *right*, Veruca, all *right*. But I can't get it for you this second. Please be patient. I'll see you have one before the day is out."

"Augustus!" shouted Mrs. Gloop. "Augustus, sweetheart, I don't think you had better do *that*." Augustus Gloop, as you might have guessed, had quietly sneaked down to the edge of the river, and he was now kneeling on the riverbank, scooping hot melted chocolate into his mouth as fast as he could.

CHAPTER SEVENTEEN

Augustus Gloop Goes up the Pipe

When Mr. Wonka turned round and saw what Augustus Gloop was doing, he cried out, "Oh, no! *Please*, Augustus, *please*! I beg of you not to do that. My chocolate must be untouched by human hands!"

"Augustus!" called out Mrs. Gloop. "Didn't you hear what the man said? Come away from that river at once!"

"This stuff is fabulous!" said Augustus, taking not the slightest notice of his mother or Mr. Wonka. "Gosh, I need a bucket to drink it properly!"

"Augustus," cried Mr. Wonka, hopping up and down and waggling his stick in the air, "you *must* come away. You are dirtying my chocolate!"

"Augustus!" cried Mrs. Gloop.

"Augustus!" cried Mr. Gloop.

But Augustus was deaf to everything except the call of his enormous stomach. He was now lying full length on the ground with his head far out over the river, lapping up the chocolate like a dog.

"Augustus!" shouted Mrs. Gloop. "You'll be giving that nasty cold of yours to about a million people all over the country!"

"Be careful, Augustus!" shouted Mr. Gloop. "You're leaning too far out!"

Mr. Gloop was absolutely right. For suddenly there was a shriek, and then a splash, and into the river went Augustus Gloop, and in one second he had disappeared under the brown surface.

"Save him!" screamed Mrs. Gloop, going white in the face, and waving her umbrella about. "He'll drown! He can't swim a yard! Save him! Save him!"

"Good heavens, woman," said Mr. Gloop, "I'm not diving in there! I've got my best suit on!"

Augustus Gloop's face came up again to the surface, painted brown with chocolate. "Help! Help! Help!" he yelled. "Fish me out!"

"Don't just *stand* there!" Mrs. Gloop screamed at Mr. Gloop. "*Do* something!"

"I *am* doing something!" said Mr. Gloop, who was now taking off his jacket and getting ready to dive into the chocolate. But while he was doing this, the wretched boy was being sucked closer and closer toward the mouth of one of the great pipes that was dangling down into the river. Then all at once, the powerful suction took hold of him completely, and he was pulled under the surface and then into the mouth of the pipe.

The crowd on the riverbank waited breathlessly to see where he would come out.

"*There he goes!*" somebody shouted, pointing upward.

And sure enough, because the pipe was made of glass, Augustus Gloop could be clearly seen shooting up inside it, head first, like a torpedo.

"Help! Murder! Police!" screamed Mrs. Gloop. "Augustus, come back at once! Where are you going?"

Augustus Gloop Goes up the Pipe

"It's a wonder to me," said Mr. Gloop, "how that pipe is big enough for him to go through it."

"It *isn't* big enough!" said Charlie Bucket. "Oh dear, look! He's slowing down!"

"So he is!" said Grandpa Joe.

"He's going to stick!" said Charlie.

"I think he is!" said Grandpa Joe.

"By golly, he *has* stuck!" said Charlie.

"It's his stomach that's done it!" said Mr. Gloop.

"He's blocked the whole pipe!" said Grandpa Joe.

"Smash the pipe!" yelled Mrs. Gloop, still waving her umbrella. "Augustus, come out of there at once!"

The watchers below could see the chocolate swishing around the boy in the pipe, and they could see it building up behind him in a solid mass, pushing against the blockage. The pressure was terrific. Something had to give. Something did give, and that something was Augustus. *WHOOF!* Up he shot again like a bullet in the barrel of a gun.

"He's disappeared!" yelled Mrs. Gloop. "Where does that pipe go to? Quick! Call the fire brigade!"

"Keep calm!" cried Mr. Wonka. "Keep calm, my dear lady, keep calm. There is no danger! No danger whatsoever! Augustus has gone on a little journey, that's all. A most interesting little journey. But he'll come out of it just fine, you wait and see."

"How can he possibly come out just fine!" snapped Mrs. Gloop. "He'll be made into marshmallows in five seconds!"

"Impossible!" cried Mr. Wonka. "Unthinkable! Inconceivable! Absurd! He could never be made into marshmallows!"

"And why not, may I ask?" shouted Mrs. Gloop.

"Because that pipe doesn't go anywhere near it! That pipe—the one Augustus went up—happens to lead directly to the room where I make a most delicious kind of strawberry-flavored chocolate-coated fudge . . ."

"Then he'll be made into strawberry-flavored chocolate-coated fudge!" screamed Mrs. Gloop. "My poor Augustus! They'll be selling him by the pound all over the country tomorrow morning!"

"Quite right," said Mr. Gloop.

"I know I'm right," said Mrs. Gloop.

"It's beyond a joke," said Mr. Gloop.

"Mr. Wonka doesn't seem to think so!" cried Mrs. Gloop. "Just look at him! He's laughing his head off! How *dare* you laugh like that when my boy's just gone up the pipe! You monster!" she shrieked, pointing her umbrella at Mr. Wonka as though she were going to run him through. "You think it's a joke, do you? You think that sucking my boy up into your Fudge Room like that is just one great big colossal joke?"

"He'll be perfectly safe," said Mr. Wonka, giggling slightly.

"He'll be chocolate fudge!" shrieked Mrs. Gloop.

"Never!" cried Mr. Wonka.

"Of course he will!" shrieked Mrs. Gloop.

"I wouldn't allow it!" cried Mr. Wonka.

"And why not?" shrieked Mrs. Gloop.

"Because the taste would be terrible," said Mr. Wonka. "Just imagine it! Augustus-flavored chocolate-coated Gloop! No one would buy it."

"They most certainly would!" cried Mr. Gloop indignantly.

"I don't want to think about it!" shrieked Mrs. Gloop.

"Nor do I," said Mr. Wonka. "And I do promise you, madam, that your darling boy is perfectly safe."

"If he's perfectly safe, then where is he?" snapped Mrs. Gloop. "Lead me to him this instant!"

Mr. Wonka turned around and clicked his fingers sharply, *click, click, click*, three times. Immediately, an Oompa-Loompa appeared, as if from nowhere, and stood beside him.

The Oompa-Loompa bowed and smiled, showing beautiful white teeth. His skin was rosy-white, his long hair was golden-brown, and the top of his head came just above the height of Mr. Wonka's knee. He wore the usual deerskin slung over his shoulder.

"Now listen to me!" said Mr. Wonka, looking down at the tiny man. "I want you to take Mr. and Mrs. Gloop up to the Fudge Room and help them to find their son, Augustus. He's just gone up the pipe."

The Oompa-Loompa took one look at Mrs. Gloop and exploded into peals of laughter.

"Oh, do be quiet!" said Mr. Wonka. "Control yourself! Pull yourself together! Mrs. Gloop doesn't think it's at all funny!"

"You can say that again!" said Mrs. Gloop.

"Go straight to the Fudge Room," Mr. Wonka said to the Oompa-Loompa, "and when you get there, take a long stick and start poking around inside the big chocolate-mixing barrel. I'm almost certain you'll find him in there. But you'd better look sharp! You'll have to hurry! If you leave him in the chocolate-mixing barrel too long, he's liable to get poured out into the fudge boiler, and that really *would* be a disaster, wouldn't it? My fudge would become *quite* uneatable!"

Mrs. Gloop let out a shriek of fury.

"I'm joking," said Mr. Wonka, giggling madly behind his beard. "I didn't mean it. Forgive me. I'm so sorry. Good-bye, Mrs. Gloop! And Mr. Gloop! Good-bye! I'll see you later . . ."

As Mr. and Mrs. Gloop and their tiny escort hurried away, the five Oompa-Loompas on the far side of the river suddenly began hopping and dancing about and beating wildly upon a number of very small drums. "Augustus Gloop!" they chanted. "Augustus Gloop! Augustus Gloop! Augustus Gloop!"

"Grandpa!" cried Charlie. "Listen to them, Grandpa! What *are* they doing?"

"Ssshh!" whispered Grandpa Joe. "I think they're going to sing us a song!"

"*Augustus Gloop!*" chanted the Oompa-Loompas.
"Augustus Gloop! Augustus Gloop!
The great big greedy nincompoop!
How long could we allow this beast
To gorge and guzzle, feed and feast
On everything he wanted to?
Great Scott! It simply wouldn't do!
However long this pig might live,
We're positive he'd never give
Even the smallest bit of fun
Or happiness to anyone.
So what we do in cases such
As this, we use the gentle touch,
And carefully we take the brat
And turn him into something that
Will give great pleasure to us all –
A doll, for instance, or a ball,
Or marbles or a rocking horse.
But this revolting boy, of course,
Was so unutterably vile,
So greedy, foul, and infantile,
He left a most disgusting taste
Inside our mouths, and so in haste
We chose a thing that, come what may,
Would take the nasty taste away.
'Come on!' we cried. 'The time is ripe
To send him shooting up the pipe!
He has to go! It has to be!'
And very soon, he's going to see
Inside the room to which he's gone
Some funny things are going on.

But don't, dear children, be alarmed;
Augustus Gloop will not be harmed,
Although, of course, we must admit
He will be altered quite a bit.
He'll be quite changed from what he's been,
When he goes through the fudge machine:
Slowly, the wheels go round and round,
The cogs begin to grind and pound;
A hundred knives go slice, slice, slice;
We add some sugar, cream, and spice;
We boil him for a minute more,
Until we're absolutely sure
That all the greed and all the gall
Is boiled away for once and all.
Then out he comes! And now! By grace!
A miracle has taken place!
This boy, who only just before
Was loathed by men from shore to shore,
This greedy brute, this louse's ear,
Is loved by people everywhere!
For who could hate or bear a grudge
Against a luscious bit of fudge?"

"I *told* you they loved singing!" cried Mr. Wonka. "Aren't they delightful? Aren't they charming? But you mustn't believe a word they said. It's all nonsense, every bit of it!"

"Are the Oompa-Loompas really joking, Grandpa?" asked Charlie.

"Of course they're joking," answered Grandpa Joe. "They *must* be joking. At least, I hope they're joking. Don't you?"

CHAPTER EIGHTEEN

Down the Chocolate River

"Off we go!" cried Mr. Wonka. "Hurry up, everybody! Follow me to the next room! And please don't worry about Augustus Gloop. He's bound to come out in the wash. They always do. We shall have to make the next part of the journey by boat! Here she comes! Look!"

A steamy mist was rising up now from the great warm chocolate river, and out of the mist there appeared suddenly a most fantastic pink boat. It was a large open row boat with a tall front and a tall back (like a Viking boat of old), and it was of such a shining sparkling glistening pink color that the whole thing looked as though it were made of bright pink glass. There were many oars on either side of it, and as the boat came closer, the watchers on the riverbank could see that the oars were being pulled by masses of Oompa-Loompas—at least ten of them to each oar.

"This is my private yacht!" cried Mr. Wonka, beaming with pleasure. "I made her by hollowing out an enormous boiled sweet! Isn't she beautiful! See how she comes cutting through the river!"

The gleaming pink boiled-sweet boat glided up to the riverbank. One hundred Oompa-Loompas rested on their oars and stared up at the visitors. Then suddenly, for some reason best known to themselves, they all burst into shrieks of laughter.

"What's so funny?" asked Violet Beauregarde.

"Oh, don't worry about *them*!" cried Mr. Wonka. "They're always laughing! They think everything's a colossal joke! Jump into the boat, all of you! Come on! Hurry up!"

Down the Chocolate River

As soon as everyone was safely in, the Oompa-Loompas pushed the boat away from the bank and began to row swiftly downriver.

"Hey, there! Mike Teavee!" shouted Mr. Wonka. "Please do not lick the boat with your tongue! It'll only make it sticky!"

"Daddy," said Veruca Salt, "I want a boat like this! I want you to buy me a big pink boiled-sweet boat exactly like Mr. Wonka's! And I want lots of Oompa-Loompas to row me about, and I want a chocolate river and I want . . . I want . . ."

"She wants a good kick in the pants," whispered Grandpa Joe to Charlie. The old man was sitting in the back of the boat and little Charlie Bucket was right beside him. Charlie was holding tightly on to his grandfather's bony old hand. He was in a whirl of excitement. Everything that he had seen so far—the great chocolate river, the waterfall, the huge sucking pipes, the minty sugar meadows, the Oompa-Loompas, the beautiful pink boat, and most of all, Mr. Willy Wonka himself—had been so astonishing that he began to wonder whether there could possibly be any more astonishments left. Where were they going now? What were they going to see? And what in the world was going to happen in the next room?

"Isn't it marvelous?" said Grandpa Joe, grinning at Charlie.

Charlie nodded and smiled up at the old man.

Suddenly, Mr. Wonka, who was sitting on Charlie's other side, reached down into the bottom of the boat, picked up a large mug, dipped it into the river, filled it with chocolate, and handed it to Charlie. "Drink this," he said. "It'll do you good! You look starved to death!"

Then Mr. Wonka filled a second mug and gave it to Grandpa Joe. "You, too," he said. "You look like a skeleton! What's the matter? Hasn't there been anything to eat in your house lately?"

"Not much," said Grandpa Joe.

Charlie put the mug to his lips, and as the rich warm creamy

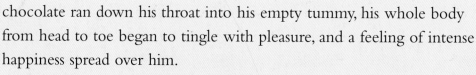

chocolate ran down his throat into his empty tummy, his whole body from head to toe began to tingle with pleasure, and a feeling of intense happiness spread over him.

"You like it?" asked Mr. Wonka.

"Oh, it's wonderful!" Charlie said.

"The creamiest loveliest chocolate I've ever tasted!" said Grandpa Joe, smacking his lips.

"That's because it's been mixed by waterfall," Mr. Wonka told him.

The boat sped on down the river. The river was getting narrower. There was some kind of a dark tunnel ahead—a great round tunnel that looked like an enormous pipe—and the river was running right into the tunnel. And so was the boat! "Row on!" shouted Mr. Wonka, jumping up and waving his stick in the air. "Full speed ahead!" And with the Oompa-Loompas rowing faster than ever, the boat shot into the pitch-dark tunnel, and all the passengers screamed with excitement.

"How can they see where they're going?" shrieked Violet Beauregarde in the darkness.

"There's no knowing where they're going!" cried Mr. Wonka, hooting with laughter.

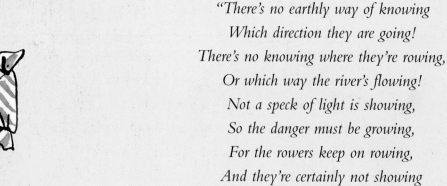

"There's no earthly way of knowing
Which direction they are going!
There's no knowing where they're rowing,
Or which way the river's flowing!
Not a speck of light is showing,
So the danger must be growing,
For the rowers keep on rowing,
And they're certainly not showing
Any signs that they are slowing . . ."

"He's gone off his rocker!" shouted one of the fathers, aghast, and the other parents joined in the chorus of frightened shouting. "He's crazy!" they shouted.

"He's balmy!"

"He's nutty!"

"He's screwy!"

"He's batty!"

"He's dippy!"

"He's dotty!"

"He's daffy!"

"He's goofy!"

"He's beany!"

"He's buggy!"

"He's wacky!"

"He's loony!"

"No, he is *not*!" said Grandpa Joe.

"Switch on the lights!" shouted Mr. Wonka. And suddenly, on came the lights and the whole tunnel was brilliantly lit up, and Charlie could see that they were indeed inside a gigantic pipe, and the great upward-curving walls of the pipe were pure white and spotlessly clean. The river of chocolate was flowing very fast inside the pipe, and the Oompa-Loompas were all rowing like mad, and the boat was rocketing along at a furious pace. Mr. Wonka was jumping up and down in the back of the boat and calling to the rowers to row faster and faster still. He seemed to love the sensation of whizzing through a white tunnel in a pink boat on a chocolate river, and he clapped his hands and laughed and kept glancing at his passengers to see if they were enjoying it as much as he.

"Look, Grandpa!" cried Charlie. "There's a door in the wall!" It was a green door and it was set into the wall of the tunnel just above the level of the river. As they flashed past it there was just enough time to read the writing on the door:

STOREROOM NUMBER 54, it said. **ALL THE CREAMS-DAIRY CREAM, WHIPPED CREAM, VIOLET CREAM, COFFEE CREAM, PINEAPPLE CREAM, VANILLA CREAM AND HAIR CREAM.**

"Hair cream?" cried Mike Teavee. "You don't use *hair cream*?"

"Row on!" shouted Mr. Wonka. "There's no time to answer silly questions!"

They streaked past a black door. **STOREROOM NUMBER 71**, it said on it. **WHIPS-ALL SHAPES AND SIZES.**

"*Whips!*" cried Veruca Salt. "What on earth do you use whips for?"

"For whipping cream, of course," said Mr. Wonka. "How can you whip cream without whips? Whipped cream isn't whipped cream at all unless it's been whipped with whips. Just as a poached egg isn't a poached egg unless it's been stolen from the woods in the dead of night! Row on, please!"

They passed a yellow door on which it said: **STOREROOM NUMBER 77, ALL THE BEANS-CACAO BEANS, COFFEE BEANS, JELLY BEANS AND HAS BEANS.**

"*Has beans?*" cried Violet Beauregarde.

"You're one yourself!" said Mr. Wonka. "There's no time for arguing! Press on, press on!" But five seconds later, when a bright red door came into sight ahead, he suddenly waved his gold-topped cane in the air and shouted, "Stop the boat!"

CHAPTER NINETEEN

The Inventing Room— Everlasting Gobstoppers and Hair Toffee

When Mr. Wonka shouted "Stop the boat!" the Oompa-Loompas jammed their oars into the river and backed water furiously. The boat stopped.

The Oompa-Loompas guided the boat alongside the red door. On the door it said, **INVENTING ROOM-PRIVATE-KEEP OUT**. Mr. Wonka took a key from his pocket, leaned over the side of the boat, and put the key in the keyhole.

"*This* is the most important room in the entire factory!" he said. "All my most secret new inventions are cooking and simmering in here! Old Fickelgruber would give his front teeth to be allowed inside just for three minutes! So would Prodnose and Slugworth and all the other rotten chocolate makers! But now, listen to me! I want no messing about when you go in! No touching, no meddling, and no tasting! Is that agreed?"

"Yes, yes!" the children cried. "We won't touch a thing!"

"Up to now," Mr. Wonka said, "nobody else, not even an Oompa-Loompa, has ever been allowed in here!" He opened the door and stepped out of the boat into the room. The four children and their parents all scrambled after him.

"Don't touch!" shouted Mr. Wonka. "And don't knock anything over!"

Charlie Bucket stared around the gigantic room in which he now found himself. The place was like a witch's kitchen! All about him black metal pots were boiling and bubbling on huge stoves, and kettles were hissing and pans were sizzling, and strange iron machines were clanking and spluttering, and there were pipes running all over the ceiling and walls, and the whole place was filled with smoke and steam and delicious rich smells.

Mr. Wonka himself had suddenly become even more excited than usual, and anyone could see that this was the room he loved best of all. He was hopping about among the saucepans and the machines like a child among his Christmas presents, not knowing which thing to look at first. He lifted the lid from a huge pot and took a sniff; then he rushed over and dipped a finger into a barrel of sticky yellow stuff and had a taste; then he skipped across to one of the machines and turned half a dozen knobs this way and that; then he peered anxiously through the glass door of a gigantic oven, rubbing his hands and cackling with delight at what he saw inside. Then he ran over to another machine, a small shiny affair that kept going *phut-phut-phut-phut-phut*, and every time it went *phut*, a large green marble dropped out of it into a basket on the floor. At least it looked like a marble.

"Everlasting Gobstoppers!" cried Mr. Wonka proudly. "They're completely new! I am inventing them for children who are given very little pocket money. You can put an Everlasting Gobstopper in your mouth and you can suck it and suck it and suck it and suck it and it will *never* get any smaller!"

"It's like gum!" cried Violet Beauregarde.

"It is *not* like gum," Mr. Wonka said. "Gum is for chewing, and if you tried chewing one of these Gobstoppers here you'd break your teeth off! And they *never* get any smaller! They *never* disappear! *NEVER!* At least I don't think they do. There's one of them being tested this very moment

in the Testing Room next door. An Oompa-Loompa is sucking it.
He's been sucking it for very nearly a year now without stopping, and
it's still just as good as ever!

"Now, over here," Mr. Wonka went on, skipping excitedly across the
room to the opposite wall, "over here I am inventing a completely new
line in toffees!" He stopped beside a large saucepan. The saucepan was
full of a thick gooey purplish treacle, boiling and bubbling. By standing
on his toes, little Charlie could just see inside it.

"That's Hair Toffee!" cried Mr. Wonka. "You eat just one tiny bit of
that, and in exactly half an hour a brand-new luscious thick silky
beautiful crop of hair will start growing out all over the top of your
head! And a moustache! And a beard!"

"A beard!" cried Veruca Salt. "Who wants a beard, for heaven's sake?"

"It would suit you very well," said Mr. Wonka, "but unfortunately the
mixture is not quite right yet. I've got it too strong. It works too well.
I tried it on an Oompa-Loompa yesterday in the Testing Room and
immediately a huge black beard started shooting out of his chin, and the
beard grew so fast that soon it was trailing all over the floor in a thick
hairy carpet. It was growing faster than we could cut it! In the end we
had to use a lawn mower to keep it in check! But I'll get the mixture
right soon! And when I do, then there'll be no excuse any more for little
boys and girls going about with bald heads!"

"But Mr. Wonka," said Mike Teavee, "little boys and girls never *do* go
about with . . ."

"Don't argue, my dear child, *please* don't argue!" cried Mr. Wonka. "It's
such a waste of precious time! Now, over *here*, if you will all step this
way, I will show you something that I am terrifically proud of. Oh, do
be careful! Don't knock anything over! Stand back!"

CHAPTER TWENTY

The Great Gum Machine

Mr. Wonka led the party over to a gigantic machine that stood in the very center of the Inventing Room. It was a mountain of gleaming metal that towered high above the children and their parents. Out of the very top of it there sprouted hundreds and hundreds of thin glass tubes, and the glass tubes all curled downward and came together in a bunch and hung suspended over an enormous round tub as big as a bath.

"Here we go!" cried Mr. Wonka, and he pressed three different buttons on the side of the machine. A second later, a mighty rumbling sound came from inside it, and the whole machine began to shake most frighteningly, and steam began hissing out of it all over, and then suddenly the watchers noticed that runny stuff was pouring down the insides of all the hundreds of little glass tubes and squirting out into the great tub below. And in every single tube the runny stuff was of a different color, so that all the colors of the rainbow (and many others as well) came sloshing and splashing into the tub. It was a lovely sight. And when the tub was nearly full, Mr. Wonka pressed another button, and immediately the runny stuff disappeared, and a whizzing whirring noise took its place; and then a giant whizzer started whizzing round inside the enormous tub, mixing up all the different colored liquids like an ice-cream soda. Gradually, the mixture began to froth. It became frothier and frothier, and it turned from blue to white to green to brown to yellow, then back to blue again.

87

"Watch!" said Mr. Wonka.

Click went the machine, and the whizzer stopped whizzing. And now there came a sort of sucking noise, and very quickly all the blue frothy mixture in the huge basin was sucked back into the stomach of the machine. There was a moment of silence. Then a few queer rumblings were heard. Then silence again. Then suddenly, the machine let out a monstrous mighty groan, and at the same moment a tiny drawer (no bigger than the drawer in a slot machine) popped out of the side of the machine, and in the drawer there lay something so small and thin and gray that everyone thought it must be a mistake. The thing looked like a little strip of gray cardboard.

The children and their parents stared at the little gray strip lying in the drawer.

"You mean that's *all*?" said Mike Teavee, disgusted.

"That's all," answered Mr. Wonka, gazing proudly at the result. "Don't you know what it is?"

There was a pause. Then suddenly, Violet Beauregarde, the silly gum-chewing girl, let out a yell of excitement. "By gum, it's *gum*!" she shrieked. "It's a stick of chewing-gum!"

"Right you are!" cried Mr. Wonka, slapping Violet hard on the back. "It's a stick of gum! It's a stick of the most *amazing* and *fabulous* and *sensational* gum in the world!"

CHAPTER TWENTY-ONE
Good-bye Violet

"This gum," Mr. Wonka went on, "is my latest, my greatest, my most fascinating invention! It's a chewing-gum meal! It's . . . it's . . . it's . . . That tiny little strip of gum lying there is a whole three-course dinner all by itself!"

"What sort of nonsense is this?" said one of the fathers.

"My dear sir!" cried Mr. Wonka, "when I start selling this gum in the shops it will change *everything*! It will be the end of all kitchens and all cooking! There will be no more shopping to do! No more buying of meat and groceries! There'll be no knives and forks at mealtimes! No plates! No washing up! No garbage! No mess! Just a little strip of Wonka's magic chewing-gum—and that's all you'll ever need at breakfast, lunch, and supper! This piece of gum I've just made happens to be tomato soup, roast beef, and blueberry pie, but you can have almost anything you want!"

"What *do* you mean, it's tomato soup, roast beef, and blueberry pie?" said Violet Beauregarde.

"If you were to start chewing it," said Mr. Wonka, "then that is exactly what you would get on the menu. It's absolutely amazing! You can actually *feel* the food going down your throat and into your tummy! And you can taste it perfectly! And it fills you up! It satisfies you! It's terrific!"

"It's utterly impossible," said Veruca Salt.

"Just so long as it's gum," shouted Violet Beauregarde, "just so long as it's a piece of gum and I can chew it, then *that's* for me!" And quickly she

took her own world-record piece of chewing-gum out of her mouth and stuck it behind her left ear. "Come on, Mr. Wonka," she said, "hand over this magic gum of yours and we'll see if the thing works."

"Now, Violet," said Mrs. Beauregarde, her mother, "don't let's do anything silly, Violet."

"I want the gum!" Violet said obstinately. "What's so silly?"

"I would rather you didn't take it," Mr. Wonka told her gently. "You see, I haven't got it *quite right* yet. There are still one or two things . . ."

"Oh, to blazes with that!" said Violet, and suddenly, before Mr. Wonka could stop her, she shot out a fat hand and grabbed the stick of gum out of the little drawer and popped it into her mouth. At once, her huge, well-trained jaws started chewing away on it like a pair of tongs.

"Don't!" said Mr. Wonka.

"Fabulous!" shouted Violet. "It's tomato soup! It's hot and creamy and delicious! I can feel it running down my throat!"

"Stop!" said Mr. Wonka. "The gum isn't ready yet! It's not right!"

"Of course it's right!" said Violet. "It's working beautifully! Oh my, what lovely soup this is!"

"Spit it out!" said Mr. Wonka.

"It's changing!" shouted Violet, chewing and grinning both at the same time. "The second course is coming up! It's roast beef! It's tender and juicy! Oh boy, what a flavor! The baked potato is marvelous, too! It's got a crispy skin and it's all filled with butter inside!"

"But how *in*-teresting, Violet," said Mrs. Beauregarde. "You are a clever girl."

"Keep chewing, baby!" said Mr. Beauregarde. "Keep right on chewing! This is a great day for the Beauregardes! Our little girl is the first person in the world to have a chewing-gum meal!"

Everybody was watching Violet Beauregarde as she stood there chewing this extraordinary gum. Little Charlie Bucket was staring at her absolutely spellbound, watching her huge rubbery lips as they pressed

and unpressed with the chewing, and Grandpa Joe stood beside him, gaping at the girl. Mr. Wonka was wringing his hands and saying, "No, no, no, no, no! It isn't ready for eating! It isn't right! You mustn't do it!"

"Blueberry pie and cream!" shouted Violet. "Here it comes! Oh my, it's perfect! It's beautiful! It's . . . it's exactly as though I'm swallowing it! It's as though I'm chewing and swallowing great big spoonfuls of the most marvelous blueberry pie in the world!"

"Good heavens, girl!" shrieked Mrs. Beauregarde suddenly, staring at Violet, "what's happening to your nose!"

"Oh, be quiet, Mother, and let me finish!" said Violet.

"It's turning blue!" screamed Mrs. Beauregarde. "Your nose is turning blue as a blueberry!"

"Your mother is right!" shouted Mr. Beauregarde. "Your whole nose has gone purple!"

"What *do* you mean?" said Violet, still chewing away.

"Your cheeks!" screamed Mrs. Beauregarde. "They're turning blue as well! So is your chin! Your whole face is turning blue!"

"Spit that gum out at once!" ordered Mr. Beauregarde.

"Mercy! Save us!" yelled Mrs. Beauregarde. "The girl's going blue and purple all over! Even her hair is changing color! Violet, you're turning violet, Violet! What *is* happening to you?"

"I *told* you I hadn't got it quite right," sighed Mr. Wonka, shaking his head sadly.

"I'll say you haven't!" cried Mrs. Beauregarde. "Just look at the girl now!"

Everybody was staring at Violet. And what a terrible, peculiar sight she was!

Goodbye Violet

Her face and hands and legs and neck, in fact the skin all over her body, as well as her great big mop of curly hair, had turned a brilliant, purplish-blue, the color of blueberry juice!

"It always goes wrong when we come to the dessert," sighed Mr. Wonka. "It's the blueberry pie that does it. But I'll get it right one day, you wait and see."

"Violet," screamed Mrs. Beauregarde, "you're swelling up!"

"I feel sick," Violet said.

"You're swelling up!" screamed Mrs. Beauregarde again.

"I feel most peculiar!" gasped Violet.

"I'm not surprised!" said Mr. Beauregarde.

"Great heavens, girl!" screeched Mrs. Beauregarde. "You're blowing up like a balloon!"

"Like a blueberry," said Mr. Wonka.

"Call a doctor!" shouted Mr. Beauregarde.

"Prick her with a pin!" said one of the other fathers.

"Save her!" cried Mrs. Beauregarde, wringing her hands.

But there was no saving her now. Her body was swelling up and changing shape at such a rate that within a minute it had turned into nothing less than an enormous round blue ball—a gigantic blueberry, in fact—and all that remained of Violet Beauregarde herself was a tiny pair of legs and a tiny pair of arms sticking out of the great round fruit and little head on top.

"It *always* happens like that," sighed Mr. Wonka. "I've tried it twenty times in the Testing Room on twenty Oompa-Loompas, and every one of them finished up as a blueberry. It's most annoying. I just can't understand it."

"But I don't want a blueberry for a daughter!" yelled Mrs. Beauregarde. "Put her back to what she was this instant!"

Mr. Wonka clicked his fingers, and ten Oompa-Loompas appeared immediately at his side.

"Roll Miss Beauregarde into the boat," he said to them, "and take her along to the Juicing Room at once."

"The *Juicing Room*?" cried Mrs. Beauregarde. "What are they going to do to her there?"

"Squeeze her," said Mr. Wonka. "We've got to squeeze the juice out of her immediately. After that, we'll just have to see how she comes out. But don't worry, my dear Mrs. Beauregarde. We'll get her repaired if it's the last thing we do. I am sorry about it all, I really am . . ."

Already the ten Oompa-Loompas were rolling the enormous blueberry across the floor of the Inventing Room toward the door that led to the chocolate river where the boat was waiting. Mr. and Mrs. Beauregarde hurried after them. The rest of the party, including little Charlie Bucket and Grandpa Joe, stood absolutely still and watched them go.

"Listen!" whispered Charlie. "Listen, Grandpa! The Oompa-Loompas in the boat outside are starting to sing!"

Goodbye Violet

The voices, one hundred of them singing together, came loud and clear into the room:

"Dear friends, we surely all agree
There's almost nothing worse to see
Than some repulsive little bum
Who's always chewing chewing-gum.
(It's very near as bad as those
Who sit around and pick the nose.)
So please believe us when we say
That chewing-gum will never pay;
This sticky habit's bound to send
The chewer to a sticky end.
Did any of you ever know
A person called Miss Bigelow?
This dreadful woman saw no wrong
In chewing, chewing all day long.
She chewed while bathing in the tub,
She chewed while dancing at her club,
She chewed in church and on the bus;
It really was quite ludicrous!
And when she couldn't find her gum,
She'd chew up the linoleum,
Or anything that happened near—
A pair of boots, the postman's ear,
Or other people's underclothes,
And once she chewed her boyfriend's nose.
She went on chewing till, at last,
Her chewing muscles grew so vast
That from her face her giant chin
Stuck out just like a violin.
For years and years she chewed away,

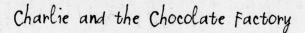

Charlie and the Chocolate Factory

Consuming fifty bits a day,
Until one summer's eve, alas,
A horrid business came to pass.
Miss Bigelow went late to bed,
For half an hour she lay and read,
Chewing and chewing all the while
Like some great clockwork crocodile.
At last, she put her gum away
Upon a special little tray,
And settled back and went to sleep—
(She managed this by counting sheep).
But now, how strange! Although she slept,
Those massive jaws of hers still kept
On chewing, chewing through the night,
Even with nothing there to bite.
They were, you see, in such a groove
They positively had to move.
And very grim it was to hear
In pitchy darkness, loud and clear,
This sleeping woman's great big trap
Opening and shutting, snap-snap-snap!
Faster and faster, chop-chop-chop,
The noise went on, it wouldn't stop.
Until at last her jaws decide
To pause and open extra wide,
And with the most tremendous chew
They bit the lady's tongue in two.
Thereafter, just from chewing-gum,
Miss Bigelow was always dumb,
And spent her life shut up in some
Disgusting sanatorium.

Goodbye Violet

And that is why we'll try so hard
To save Miss Violet Beauregarde
From suffering an equal fate.
She's still quite young. It's not too late,
Provided she survives the cure.
We hope she does. We can't be sure."

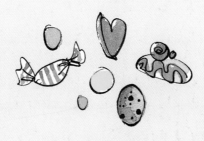

CHAPTER TWENTY-TWO
Along the Corridor

"Well, well, well," sighed Mr. Willy Wonka, "two naughty little children gone. Three good little children left. I think we'd better get out of this room quickly before we lose anyone else!"

"But Mr. Wonka," said Charlie Bucket anxiously, "will Violet Beauregarde *ever* be all right again or will she always be a blueberry?"

"They'll de-juice her in no time flat!" declared Mr. Wonka. "They'll roll her into the de-juicing machine, and she'll come out just as thin as a whistle!"

"But will she still be blue all over?" asked Charlie.

"She'll be *purple*!" cried Mr. Wonka. "A fine rich purple from head to toe! But there you are! That's what comes from chewing disgusting gum all day long!"

"If you think gum is so disgusting," said Mike Teavee, "then why do you make it in your factory?"

"I do wish you wouldn't mumble," said Mr. Wonka. "I can't hear a word you're saying. Come on! Off we go! Hurry up! Follow me! We're going into the corridors again!" And so saying, Mr. Wonka scuttled across to the far end of the Inventing Room and went out through a small secret door hidden behind a lot of pipes and stoves. The three remaining children—Veruca Salt, Mike Teavee, and Charlie Bucket—together with the five remaining grown-ups, followed after him.

Charlie Bucket saw that they were now back in one of those long pink corridors with many other pink corridors leading out of it. Mr.

Along the Corridor

Wonka was rushing along in front, turning left and right and right and left, and Grandpa Joe was saying, "Keep a good hold of my hand, Charlie. It would be terrible to get lost in here."

Mr. Wonka was saying, "No time for any more messing about! We'll never get *anywhere* at the rate we've been going!" And on he rushed, down the endless pink corridors, with his black top hat perched on the top of his head and his plum-colored velvet coattails flying out behind him like a flag in the wind.

They passed a door in the wall. "No time to go in!" shouted Mr. Wonka. "Press on! Press on!"

They passed another door, then another and another. There were doors every twenty paces or so along the corridor now, and they all had something written on them, and strange clanking noises were coming from behind several of them, and delicious smells came wafting through the keyholes, and sometimes little jets of colored steam shot out from the cracks underneath.

Grandpa Joe and Charlie were half running and half walking to keep

up with Mr. Wonka, but they were able to read what it said on quite a few of the doors as they hurried by. **EATABLE MARSHMALLOW PILLOWS**, it said on one.

"Marshmallow pillows are terrific!" shouted Mr. Wonka as he dashed by. "They'll be all the rage when I get them into the shops! No time to go in, though! No time to go in!"

LICKABLE WALLPAPER FOR NURSERIES, it said on the next door.

"Lovely stuff, lickable wallpaper!" cried Mr. Wonka, rushing past. "It has pictures of fruits on it–bananas, apples, oranges, grapes, pineapples, strawberries and snozzberries . . ."

"*Snozzberries?*" said Mike Teavee.

"Don't interrupt!" said Mr. Wonka. "The wallpaper has pictures of all these fruits printed on it, and when you lick the picture of a banana, it tastes of banana. When you lick a strawberry, it tastes of strawberry. And when you lick a snozzberry, it tastes just exactly like a snozzberry . . ."

"But what *does* a snozzberry taste like?"

"You're mumbling again," said Mr. Wonka. "Speak louder next time. On we go! Hurry up!"

HOT ICE CREAMS FOR COLD DAYS, it said on the next door.

"*Extremely* useful in the winter," said Mr. Wonka, rushing on. "Hot ice cream warms you up no end in freezing weather. I also make hot ice cubes for putting in hot drinks. Hot ice cubes make hot drinks hotter."

COWS THAT GIVE CHOCOLATE MILK, it said on the next door.

"Ah, my pretty little cows!" cried Mr. Wonka. "How I love those cows!"

"But why can't we *see* them?" asked Veruca Salt. "Why do we have to go rushing on past all these lovely rooms?"

"We shall stop in time!" called out Mr. Wonka. "Don't be so madly impatient!"

FIZZY LIFTING DRINKS, it said on the next door.

"Oh, those are fabulous!" cried Mr. Wonka. "They fill you with bubbles, and the bubbles are full of a special kind of gas, and this gas is so terrifically *lifting* that it lifts you right off the ground just like a balloon, and up you go until your head hits the ceiling–and there you stay."

"But how do you come down again?" asked little Charlie.

"You do a burp, of course," said Mr. Wonka. "You do a great big long rude burp, and *up* comes the gas and down comes you! But don't drink it outdoors! There's no knowing how high up you'll be carried if you do that. I gave some to an old Oompa-Loompa once out in the backyard and he went up and up and disappeared out of sight! It was very sad. I never saw him again."

"He should have burped," Charlie said.

"Of course he should have burped," said Mr. Wonka. "I stood there shouting, 'Burp, you silly twit, burp, or you'll never come down again!' But he didn't or couldn't or wouldn't, I don't know which. Maybe he was too polite. He must be on the moon by now."

On the next door, it said, **SQUARE SWEETS THAT LOOK ROUND**.

"Wait!" cried Mr. Wonka, skidding suddenly to a halt. "I am very proud of my square sweets that look round. Let's take a peek."

CHAPTER TWENTY-THREE

Square Sweets That Look Round

Everybody stopped and crowded to the door. The top half of the door was made of glass. Grandpa Joe lifted Charlie up so that he could get a better view, and looking in, Charlie saw a long table, and on the table there were rows and rows of small white square-shaped sweets. The sweets looked very much like square sugar lumps—except that each of them had a funny little pink face painted on one side. At the end of the table, a number of Oompa-Loompas were busily painting more faces on more sweets.

"There you are!" cried Mr. Wonka. "Square sweets that look round!"

"They don't look round to me," said Mike Teavee.

"They look square," said Veruca Salt. "They look completely square."

"But they *are* square," said Mr. Wonka. "I never said they weren't."

"You said they were *round*!" said Veruca Salt.

"I never said anything of the sort," said Mr. Wonka. "I said they *looked* round."

"But they *don't* look round!" said Veruca Salt. "They look square!"

"They look round," insisted Mr. Wonka.

"They most certainly do not look round!" cried Veruca Salt.

"Veruca, darling," said Mrs. Salt, "pay no attention to Mr. Wonka! He's lying to you!"

"My dear old fish," said Mr. Wonka, "go and boil your head!"

"How dare you speak to me like that!" shouted Mrs. Salt.

"Oh, do shut up," said Mr. Wonka. "Now watch this!"

He took a key from his pocket, and unlocked the door, and flung it open . . . and suddenly . . . at the sound of the door opening, all the rows of little square sweets looked quickly round to see who was coming in. The tiny faces actually turned toward the door and stared at Mr. Wonka.

"There you are!" he cried triumphantly. "They're looking round! There's no argument about it! They are square sweets that look round!"

"By golly, he's right!" said Grandpa Joe.

"Come on!" said Mr. Wonka, starting off down the corridor again. "On we go! We mustn't dawdle!"

BUTTERSCOTCH AND BUTTERGIN, it said on the next door they passed.

"Now *that* sounds a bit more interesting," said Mr. Salt, Veruca's father.

"Glorious stuff!" said Mr. Wonka. "The Oompa-Loompas all adore it. It makes them tiddly. Listen! You can hear them in there now, whooping it up."

Shrieks of laughter and snatches of singing could be heard coming through the closed door.

"They're drunk as lords," said Mr. Wonka. "They're drinking butterscotch and soda. They like that best of all. Buttergin and tonic is also very popular. Follow me, please! We really mustn't keep stopping like this." He turned left. He turned right. They came to a long flight of stairs. Mr. Wonka slid down the banisters. The three children did the same. Mrs. Salt and Mrs. Teavee, the only women now left in the party, were getting very out of breath. Mrs. Salt was a great fat creature with short legs, and she was blowing like a rhinoceros. "This way!" cried Mr. Wonka, turning left at the bottom of the stairs.

"Go *slower!*" panted Mrs. Salt.

"Impossible," said Mr. Wonka. "We should never get there in time if I did."

"Get where?" asked Veruca Salt.

"Never you mind," said Mr. Wonka. "You just wait and see."

CHAPTER TWENTY-FOUR

Veruca in the Nut Room

Mr. Wonka rushed on down the corridor. **THE NUT ROOM**, it said on the next door they came to.

"All right," said Mr. Wonka, "stop here for a moment and catch your breath, and take a peek through the glass panel of this door. But don't go in! Whatever you do, don't go into **THE NUT ROOM**! If you go in, you'll disturb the squirrels!"

Everyone crowded around the door.

"Oh look, Grandpa, look!" cried Charlie.

"Squirrels!" shouted Veruca Salt.

"Crikey!" said Mike Teavee.

It was an amazing sight. One hundred squirrels were seated upon high stools around a large table. On the table, there were mounds and mounds of walnuts, and the squirrels were all working away like mad, shelling the walnuts at a tremendous speed.

"These squirrels are specially trained for getting the nuts out of walnuts," Mr. Wonka explained.

"Why use squirrels?" Mike Teavee asked. "Why not use Oompa-Loompas?"

"Because," said Mr. Wonka, "Oompa-Loompas can't get walnuts out of walnut shells in one piece. They always break them in two. Nobody except squirrels can get walnuts *whole* out of walnut shells every time. It is extremely difficult. But in my factory, I insist upon only whole walnuts. Therefore I have to have squirrels to do the job. Aren't they wonderful, the way they get those nuts out! And see how they first tap each walnut with their knuckles to be sure it's not a bad one! If it's bad, it makes a hollow sound, and they don't bother to open it. They just throw it down the garbage chute. There! Look! Watch that squirrel nearest to us! I think he's got a bad one now!"

They watched the little squirrel as he tapped the walnut shell with his knuckles. He cocked his head to one side, listening intently, then suddenly he threw the nut over his shoulder into a large hole in the floor.

"Hey, Mummy!" shouted Veruca Salt suddenly. "I've decided I want a squirrel! Get me one of those squirrels!"

"Don't be silly, sweetheart," said Mrs. Salt. "These all belong to Mr. Wonka."

"I don't care about that!" shouted Veruca. "I want one. All I've *got* at home is two dogs and four cats and six bunny rabbits and two parakeets and three canaries and a green parrot and a turtle and a bowl of goldfish and a cage of white mice and a silly old hamster! I want a *squirrel!*"

"All right, my pet," Mrs. Salt said soothingly. "Mummy'll get you a squirrel just as soon as she possibly can."

"But I don't want *any* old squirrel!" Veruca shouted. "I want a *trained* squirrel!"

At this point, Mr. Salt, Veruca's father, stepped forward. "Very well, Wonka," he said importantly, taking out a wallet full of money, "how much d'you want for one of these squirrels? Name your price."

"They're not for sale," Mr. Wonka answered. "She can't have one."

"Who says I can't!" shouted Veruca. "I'm going in to get myself one this very minute!"

"Don't!" said Mr. Wonka quickly, but he was too late. The girl had already thrown open the door and rushed in.

Veruca in the Nut Room

The moment she entered the room, one hundred squirrels stopped what they were doing and turned their heads and stared at her with small black beady eyes.

Veruca Salt stopped also, and stared back at them. Then her gaze fell upon a pretty little squirrel sitting nearest to her at the end of the table. The squirrel was holding a walnut in its paws.

"All right," Veruca said, "I'll have *you*!"

She reached out her hands to grab the squirrel . . . but as she did so . . . in that first split second when her hands started to go forward, there was a sudden flash of movement in the room, like a flash of brown lightning, and every single squirrel around the table took a flying leap toward her and landed on her body.

Twenty-five of them caught hold of her right arm, and pinned it down.

Twenty-five more caught hold of her left arm, and pinned that down.

Twenty-five caught hold of her right leg and anchored it to the ground.

Twenty-*four* caught hold of her left leg.

And the one remaining squirrel (obviously the leader of them all) climbed up on to her shoulder and started tap-tap-tapping the wretched girl's head with its knuckles.

"Save her!" screamed Mrs. Salt. "Veruca! Come back! What are they *doing* to her?"

"They're testing her to see if she's a bad nut," said Mr. Wonka. "You watch."

Veruca struggled furiously, but the squirrels held her tight and she couldn't move. The squirrel on her shoulder went tap-tap-tapping the side of her head with his knuckles.

Then all at once, the squirrels pulled Veruca to the ground and started carrying her across the floor.

"My goodness, she *is* a bad nut after all," said Mr. Wonka. "Her head must have sounded quite hollow."

Veruca kicked and screamed, but it was no use. The tiny strong paws held her tightly and she couldn't escape.

"Where are they taking her?" shrieked Mrs. Salt.

"She's going where all the other bad nuts go," said Mr. Willy Wonka. "Down the garbage chute."

"By golly, she *is* going down the chute!" said Mr. Salt, staring through the glass door at his daughter.

"Then save her!" cried Mrs. Salt.

"Too late," said Mr. Wonka. "She's gone!"

And indeed she had.

"But where?" shrieked Mrs. Salt, flapping her arms. "What happens to the bad nuts? Where does the chute go to?"

"That *particular* chute," Mr. Wonka told her, "runs directly into the great big main garbage pipe which carries away all the garbage from every part of the factory—all the floor sweepings and potato peelings and rotten cabbages and fish heads and stuff like that."

"Who eats fish and cabbage and potatoes in *this* factory, I'd like to know?" said Mike Teavee.

"I do, of course," answered Mr. Wonka. "You don't think I live on cacao beans, do you?"

"But . . . but . . . but . . ." shrieked Mrs. Salt, "where does the great big pipe go to in the end?"

"Why, to the furnace, of course," Mr. Wonka said calmly. "To the incinerator."

Mrs. Salt opened her huge red mouth and started to scream.

"Don't worry," said Mr. Wonka, "there's always a chance that they've decided not to light it today."

"A *chance*!" yelled Mrs. Salt. "My darling Veruca! She'll . . . she'll . . . she'll be sizzled like a sausage!"

"Quite right, my dear," said Mr. Salt. "Now see here, Wonka," he added, "I think you've gone *just* a shade too far this time, I do indeed. My daughter may be a bit of a frump—I don't mind admitting it—but that doesn't mean you can roast her to a crisp. I'll have you know I'm extremely cross about this, I really am."

"Oh, don't be cross, my dear sir!" said Mr. Wonka. "I expect she'll turn up again sooner or later. She may not even have gone down at all. She may be stuck in the chute just below the entrance hole, and if *that's* the case, all you'll have to do is go in and pull her up again."

Hearing this, both Mr. and Mrs. Salt dashed into the Nut Room and ran over to the hole in the floor and peered in.

"Veruca!" shouted Mrs. Salt. "Are you down there!"

There was no answer.

Mrs. Salt bent further forward to get a closer look. She was now kneeling right on the edge of the hole with her head down and her enormous behind sticking up in the air like a giant mushroom. It was a dangerous position to be in. She needed only one tiny little push . . . one gentle nudge in the right place . . . and *that* is exactly what the squirrels gave her! Over she toppled, into the hole head first, screeching like a parrot.

"Good gracious me!" said Mr. Salt, as he watched his fat wife go tumbling down the hole, "what a lot of garbage there's going to be today!" He saw her disappearing into the darkness. "What's it like down there, Angina?" he called out. He leaned further forward.

The squirrels rushed up behind him . . .

"Help!" he shouted.

But he was already toppling forward, and down the chute he went,

just as his wife had done before him—and his daughter.

"Oh *dear*!" cried Charlie, who was watching with the others through the door, "what on earth's going to happen to them now?"

"I expect someone will catch them at the bottom of the chute," said Mr. Wonka.

"But what about the great fiery incinerator?" asked Charlie.

"They only light it every other day," said Mr. Wonka. "Perhaps this is one of the days when they let it go out. You never know . . . they might be lucky . . ."

"Ssshh!" said Grandpa Joe. "Listen! Here comes another song!"

From far away down the corridor came the beating of drums. Then the singing began.

Charlie and the Chocolate Factory

"Veruca Salt!" sang the Oompa-Loompas.
"Veruca Salt, the little brute,
Has just gone down the garbage chute
(And as we very rightly thought
That in a case like this we ought
To see the thing completely through,
We've polished off her parents, too).
Down goes Veruca! Down the drain!
And here, perhaps, we should explain
That she will meet, as she descends,
A rather different set of friends
To those that she has left behind—
These won't be nearly so refined.
A fish head, for example, cut
This morning from a halibut.
'Hello! Good morning! How d'you do?
How nice to meet you! How are you?'
And then a little further down
A mass of others gather round:
A bacon rind, some rancid lard,
A loaf of bread gone stale and hard,
A steak that nobody could chew,
An oyster from an oyster stew,
Some liverwurst so old and gray
One smelled it from a mile away,
A rotten nut, a reeky pear,
A thing the cat left on the stair,
And lots of other things as well,
Each with a rather horrid smell.
These are Veruca's newfound friends
That she will meet as she descends,

Veruca in the Nut Room

And this *is the price she has to pay*
For going so very far astray.
But now, my dears, we think you might
Be wondering—is it really right
That every single bit of blame
And all the scolding and the shame
Should fall upon Veruca Salt?
Is she *the only one at fault?*
For though she's spoiled, and dreadfully so,
A girl can't spoil herself, you know.
Who *spoiled her, then? Ah, who indeed?*
Who *pandered to her every need?*
Who *turned her into such a brat?*
Who *are the culprits? Who did that?*
Alas! You needn't look so far
To find out who these sinners are.
They are (and this is very sad)
Her loving parents, MUM and DAD.
And that is why we're glad they fell
Into the garbage chute as well."

CHAPTER TWENTY-FIVE
The Great Glass Elevator

"I've never seen anything like it!" cried Mr. Wonka. "The children are disappearing like rabbits! But you mustn't worry about it! They'll *all* come out in the wash!"

Mr. Wonka looked at the little group that stood beside him in the corridor. There were only two children left now—Mike Teavee and Charlie Bucket. And there were three grown-ups, Mr. and Mrs. Teavee and Grandpa Joe. "Shall we move on?" Mr. Wonka asked.

"Oh, yes!" cried Charlie and Grandpa Joe, both together.

"My feet are getting tired," said Mike Teavee. "I want to watch television."

"If you're tired then we'd better take the elevator," said Mr. Wonka. "It's over here. Come on! In we go!" He skipped across the passage to a pair of double doors. The doors slid open. The two children and the grown-ups went in.

"Now then," cried Mr. Wonka, "which button shall we press first? Take your pick!"

Charlie Bucket stared around him in astonishment. This was the craziest elevator he had ever seen. There were buttons everywhere! The walls, and even the *ceiling*, were covered all over with rows and rows and rows of small, black push buttons! There must have been a thousand of them on each wall, and another thousand on the ceiling! And now Charlie noticed that every single button had a tiny printed label beside it

telling you which room you would be taken to if you pressed it.

"This isn't just an ordinary up-and-down elevator!" announced Mr. Wonka proudly. "This elevator can go sideways and longways and slantways and any other way you can think of! It can visit any single room in the whole factory, no matter where it is! You simply press the button . . . and *zing*! . . . you're off!"

"*Fantastic!*" murmured Grandpa Joe. His eyes were shining with excitement as he stared at the rows of buttons.

"The whole elevator is made of thick, clear glass!" Mr. Wonka declared. "Walls, doors, ceiling, floor, everything is made of glass so that you can see out!"

"But there's nothing to see," said Mike Teavee.

"Choose a button!" said Mr. Wonka. "The two children may press one button each. So take your pick! Hurry up! In every room, something delicious and wonderful is being made."

Quickly, Charlie started reading some of the labels alongside the buttons.

THE ROCK-CANDY MINE–10,000 FEET DEEP. , it said on one.

COKERNUT-ICE SKATING RINKS. , it said on another.

Then . . . STRAWBERRY-JUICE WATER PISTOLS.

TOFFEE-APPLE TREES FOR PLANTING OUT IN YOUR GARDEN–ALL SIZES.

EXPLODING SWEETS FOR YOUR ENEMIES.

LUMINOUS LOLLIES FOR EATING IN BED AT NIGHT.

MINT JUJUBES FOR THE BOY NEXT DOOR–THEY'LL GIVE HIM GREEN TEETH FOR A MONTH.

CAVITY-FILLING CARAMELS–NO MORE DENTISTS.

STICKJAW FOR TALKATIVE PARENTS.

WRIGGLE-SWEETS THAT WRIGGLE DELIGHTFULLY IN YOUR TUMMY AFTER SWALLOWING.

INVISIBLE CHOCOLATE BARS FOR EATING IN CLASS.

SUGAR-COATED PENCILS FOR SUCKING.

FIZZY LEMONADE SWIMMING POOLS.

MAGIC HAND-FUDGE-WHEN YOU HOLD IT IN YOUR HAND, YOU TASTE IT IN YOUR MOUTH.

RAINBOW DROPS-SUCK THEM AND YOU CAN SPIT IN SIX DIFFERENT COLORS.

"Come on, come on!" cried Mr. Wonka. "We can't wait all day!"

"Isn't there a *Television Room* in all this lot?" asked Mike Teavee.

"Certainly there's a television room," Mr. Wonka said. "That button over there." He pointed with his finger. Everybody looked.

TELEVISION CHOCOLATE. , it said on the tiny label beside the button.

"*Whoopee!*" shouted Mike Teavee. "That's for me!" He stuck out his thumb and pressed the button. Instantly, there was a tremendous whizzing noise. The doors clanged shut and the elevator leaped away as though it had been stung by a wasp. But it leapt *sideways*! And all the passengers (except Mr. Wonka, who was holding on to a strap from the ceiling) were flung off their feet on to the floor.

"Get up, get up!" cried Mr. Wonka, roaring with laughter. But just as they were staggering to their feet, the elevator changed direction and swerved violently round a corner. And over they went once more.

"Help!" shouted Mrs. Teavee.

"Take my hand, madam," said Mr. Wonka gallantly. "There you are! Now grab this strap! Everybody grab a strap. The journey's not over yet!"

Old Grandpa Joe staggered to his feet and caught hold of a strap. Little Charlie, who couldn't possibly reach as high as that, put his arms around Grandpa Joe's legs and hung on tight.

The elevator rushed on at the speed of a rocket. Now it was beginning to climb. It was shooting up and up and up on a steep slanty course as if it were climbing a very steep hill. Then suddenly, as though it had come to the top of the hill and gone over a precipice, it dropped like

a stone and Charlie felt his tummy coming right up into his throat, and Grandpa Joe shouted, "Yippee! Here we go!" and Mrs. Teavee cried out, "The rope has broken! We're going to crash!" And Mr. Wonka said, "Calm yourself, my dear lady," and patted her comfortingly on the arm. And then Grandpa Joe looked down at Charlie who was clinging to his legs, and he said, "Are you all right, Charlie?" Charlie shouted, "I love it! It's like being on a roller coaster!" And through the glass walls of the

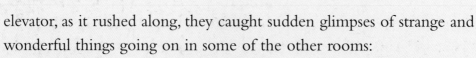

elevator, as it rushed along, they caught sudden glimpses of strange and wonderful things going on in some of the other rooms:

An enormous spout with brown sticky stuff oozing out of it on to the floor . . .

A great, craggy mountain made entirely of fudge, with Oompa-Loompas (all roped together for safety) hacking huge hunks of fudge out of its sides . . .

A machine with white powder spraying out of it like a snowstorm . . .

A lake of hot caramel with steam coming off it . . .

A village of Oompa-Loompas, with tiny houses and streets and hundreds of Oompa-Loompa children no more than four inches high playing in the streets . . .

And now the elevator began flattening out again, but it seemed to be going faster than ever, and Charlie could hear the scream of the wind outside as it hurtled forward . . . and it twisted . . . and it turned . . . and it went up . . . and it went down . . . and . . .

"I'm going to be sick!" yelled Mrs. Teavee, turning green in the face.

"Please don't be sick," said Mr. Wonka.

"Try and stop me!" said Mrs. Teavee.

"Then you'd better take this," said Mr. Wonka, and he swept his magnificent black top hat off his head, and held it out, upside down, in front of Mrs. Teavee's mouth.

"Make this awful thing stop!" ordered Mr. Teavee.

"Can't do that," said Mr. Wonka. "It won't stop till we get there. I only hope no one's using the *other* elevator at this moment."

"What other elevator?" screamed Mrs. Teavee.

"The one that goes the opposite way on the same track as this one," said Mr. Wonka.

"Holy mackerel!" cried Mr. Teavee. "You mean we might have a collision?"

"I've always been lucky so far," said Mr. Wonka.

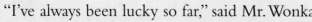

"Now I *am* going to be sick!" yelled Mrs. Teavee.

"No, no!" said Mr. Wonka. "Not now! We're nearly there! Don't spoil my hat!"

The next moment, there was a screaming of brakes, and the elevator began to slow down. Then it stopped altogether.

"Some ride!" said Mr. Teavee, wiping his great sweaty face with a handkerchief.

"Never again!" gasped Mrs. Teavee. And then the doors of the elevator slid open and Mr. Wonka said, "Just a minute now! Listen to me! I want everybody to be very careful in this room. There is dangerous stuff around in here and you *must not* tamper with it."

CHAPTER TWENTY-SIX

The Television-Chocolate Room

The Teavee family, together with Charlie and Grandpa Joe, stepped out of the lift into a room so dazzlingly bright and dazzlingly white that they screwed up their eyes in pain and stopped walking. Mr. Wonka handed each of them a pair of dark glasses and said, "Put these on quick! And don't take them off in here whatever you do! This light could blind you!"

As soon as Charlie had his dark glasses on, he was able to look around him in comfort. He saw a long narrow room. The room was painted white all over. Even the floor was white, and there wasn't a speck of dust anywhere. From the ceiling, huge lamps hung down and bathed the room in a brilliant blue-white light. The room was completely bare except at the far ends. At one of these ends there was an enormous camera on wheels, and a whole army of Oompa-Loompas was clustering around it, oiling its joints and adjusting its knobs and polishing its great glass lens. The Oompa-Loompas were all dressed in the most extraordinary way. They were wearing bright-red space suits, complete with helmets and goggles—at least they looked like space suits—and they were working in complete silence. Watching them, Charlie experienced a queer sense of danger. There was something dangerous about this whole business, and the Oompa-Loompas knew it. There was no chattering or singing among them here, and they moved about over the huge black camera slowly and carefully in their scarlet space suits.

The Television-Chocolate Room

At the other end of the room, about fifty paces away from the camera, a single Oompa-Loompa (also wearing a space suit) was sitting at a black table gazing at the screen of a very large television set.

"Here we go!" cried Mr. Wonka, hopping up and down with excitement. "This is the Testing Room for my very latest and greatest invention–Television Chocolate!"

"But what *is* Television Chocolate?" asked Mike Teavee.

"Good heavens, child, stop interrupting me!" said Mr. Wonka. "It works by television. I don't like television myself. I suppose it's all right in small doses, but children never seem to be able to take it in small doses. They want to sit there all day long staring and staring at the screen . . ."

"That's me!" said Mike Teavee.

"Shut up!" said Mr. Teavee.

"Thank you," said Mr. Wonka. "I shall now tell you how this amazing television set of mine works. But first of all, do you know how ordinary television works? It is very simple. At one end, where the picture is being taken, you have a large movie camera and you start photographing something. The photographs are then split up into millions of tiny little pieces which are so small that you can't see them, and these little pieces are shot out into the sky by electricity. In the sky, they go whizzing around all over the place until suddenly they hit the antenna on the roof of somebody's house. They then go flashing down the wire that leads right into the back of the television set, and in there they get jiggled and joggled around until at last every single one of those millions of tiny pieces is fitted back into its right place (just like a jigsaw puzzle), and presto!–the photograph appears on the screen . . ."

"That isn't *exactly* how it works," Mike Teavee said.

"I am a little deaf in my left ear," Mr. Wonka said. "You must forgive me if I don't hear everything you say."

"I said, that isn't *exactly* how it works!" shouted Mike Teavee.

"You're a nice boy," Mr. Wonka said, "but you talk too much. Now

then! The very first time I saw ordinary television working, I was struck by a tremendous idea. 'Look here!' I shouted. 'If these people can break up a *photograph* into millions of pieces and send the pieces whizzing through the air and then put them together again at the other end, why can't I do the same thing with a bar of chocolate? Why can't *I* send a real bar of chocolate whizzing through the air in tiny pieces and then put the pieces together at the other end, all ready to be eaten?' "

"Impossible!" said Mike Teavee.

"You think so?" cried Mr. Wonka. "Well, watch this! I shall now send a bar of my very best chocolate from one end of this room to the other—by television! Get ready, there! Bring in the chocolate!"

Immediately, six Oompa-Loompas marched forward carrying on their shoulders the most enormous bar of chocolate Charlie had ever seen. It was about the size of the mattress he slept on at home.

"It has to be big," Mr. Wonka explained, "because whenever you send

something by television, it always comes out much smaller than it was when it went in. Even with *ordinary* television, when you photograph a big man, he never comes out on your screen any taller than a pencil, does he? Here we go, then! Get ready! *No, no! Stop! Hold everything!* You there! Mike Teavee! Stand back! You're too close to the camera! There are dangerous rays coming out of that thing! They could break you up into a million tiny pieces in one second! That's why the Oompa-Loompas are wearing space suits! The suits protect them! All right! That's better! Now, then! *Switch on!*"

One of the Oompa-Loompas caught hold of a large switch and pulled it down.

There was a blinding flash.

"The chocolate's gone!" shouted Grandpa Joe, waving his arms.

He was quite right! The whole enormous bar of chocolate had disappeared completely into thin air!

"It's on its way!" cried Mr. Wonka. "It is now rushing through the air above our heads in a million tiny pieces. Quick! Come over here!" He dashed over to the other end of the room where the large television set was standing, and the others followed him. "Watch the screen!" he cried. "Here it comes! Look!"

The screen flickered and lit up. Then suddenly, a small bar of chocolate appeared in the middle of the screen.

"Take it!" shouted Mr. Wonka, growing more and more excited.

"How can you take it?" asked Mike Teavee, laughing. "It's just a picture on a television screen!"

"Charlie Bucket!" cried Mr. Wonka. *"You* take it! Reach out and grab it!"

Charlie put out his hand and touched the screen, and suddenly, miraculously, the bar of chocolate came away in his fingers. He was so surprised he nearly dropped it.

"Eat it!" shouted Mr. Wonka. "Go on and eat it! It'll be delicious! It's the same bar! It's got smaller on the journey, that's all!"

"It's absolutely fantastic!" gasped Grandpa Joe. "It's . . . it's . . . it's a miracle!"

"Just imagine," cried Mr. Wonka, "when I start using this across the country . . . you'll be sitting at home watching television and suddenly a commercial will flash on to the screen and a voice will say, 'EAT WONKA'S CHOCOLATES! THEY'RE THE BEST IN THE WORLD! IF YOU DON'T BELIEVE US, TRY ONE FOR YOURSELF–*NOW*!' And you simply reach out and take one! How about that, eh?"

"Terrific!" cried Grandpa Joe. "It will change the world!"

CHAPTER TWENTY-SEVEN

Mike Teavee is Sent by Television

Mike Teavee was even more excited than Grandpa Joe at seeing a bar of chocolate being sent by television. "But Mr. Wonka," he shouted, "can you send *other things* through the air in the same way? Breakfast cereal, for instance?"

"Oh, my sainted aunt!" cried Mr. Wonka. "Don't mention that disgusting stuff in front of me! Do you know what breakfast cereal is made of? It's made of all those little curly wooden shavings you find in pencil sharpeners!"

"But could you send it by television if you wanted to, as you do chocolate?" asked Mike Teavee.

"Of course I could!"

"And what about people?" asked Mike Teavee. "Could you send a real live person from one place to another in the same way?"

"A *person*!" cried Mr. Wonka. "Are you off your rocker?"

"But *could* it be done?"

"Good heavens, child, I really don't know . . . I suppose it *could* . . . yes. I'm pretty sure it could . . . of course it could . . . I wouldn't like to risk it, though . . . it might have some very nasty results . . ."

But Mike Teavee was already off and running. The moment he heard Mr. Wonka saying, "I'm pretty sure it could . . . of course it could," he turned away and started running as fast as he could toward the other end of the room where the great camera was standing. "Look at me!" he shouted as he ran. "I'm going to be the first person in the world to be sent by television!"

"*No, no, no, no!*" cried Mr. Wonka.

"Mike!" screamed Mrs. Teavee. "Stop! Come back! You'll be turned into a million tiny pieces!"

But there was no stopping Mike Teavee now. The crazy boy rushed on, and when he reached the enormous camera, he jumped straight for the switch, scattering Oompa-Loompas right and left as he went.

"See you later, alligator!" he shouted, and he pulled down the switch, and as he did so, he leaped out into the full glare of the mighty lens.

There was a blinding flash.

Then there was silence.

Then Mrs. Teavee ran forward . . . but she stopped dead in the middle of the room . . . and she stood there . . . she stood staring at the place where her son had been . . . and her great red mouth opened wide and she screamed, "He's gone! He's gone!"

"Great heavens, he *has* gone!" shouted Mr. Teavee.

Mr. Wonka hurried forward and placed a hand gently on Mrs. Teavee's shoulder. "We shall have to hope for the best," he said. "We must pray that your little boy will come out unharmed at the other end."

"Mike!" screamed Mrs. Teavee, clasping her head in her hands. "Where are you?"

"I'll tell you where he is," said Mr. Teavee, "he's whizzing around above our heads in a million tiny pieces!"

"Don't talk about it!" wailed Mrs. Teavee.

"We must watch the television set," said Mr. Wonka. "He may come through any moment."

Mr. and Mrs. Teavee and Grandpa Joe and little Charlie and Mr. Wonka all gathered round the television and stared tensely at the screen. The screen was quite blank.

"He's taking a heck of a long time to come across," said Mr. Teavee, wiping his brow.

"Oh dear, oh dear," said Mr. Wonka, "I do hope that no part of him gets left behind."

"What on earth do you mean?" asked Mr. Teavee sharply.

"I don't wish to alarm you," said Mr. Wonka, "but it does sometimes happen that only about half the little pieces find their way into the television set. It happened last week. I don't know why, but the result was that only half a bar of chocolate came through."

Mrs. Teavee let out a scream of horror. "You mean only a half of Mike is coming back to us?" she cried.

"Let's hope it's the top half," said Mr. Teavee.

"Hold everything!" said Mr. Wonka. "Watch the screen! Something's happening!"

The screen had suddenly begun to flicker.

Then some wavy lines appeared.

Mr. Wonka adjusted one of the knobs and the wavy lines went away.

And now, very slowly, the screen began to get brighter and brighter.

"Here he comes!" yelled Mr. Wonka. "Yes, that's him all right!"

"Is he all in one piece?" cried Mrs. Teavee.

"I'm not sure," said Mr. Wonka. "It's too early to tell."

Faintly at first, but becoming clearer and clearer every second, the picture of Mike Teavee appeared on the screen. He was standing up and waving at the audience and grinning from ear to ear.

"But he's a midget!" shouted Mr. Teavee.

"Mike," cried Mrs. Teavee, "are you all right? Are there any bits of you missing?"

"Isn't he going to get any bigger?" shouted Mr. Teavee.

"Talk to me, Mike!" cried Mrs. Teavee. "Say something! Tell me you're all right!"

A tiny little voice, no louder than the squeaking of a mouse, came out of the television set. "Hi, Mum!" it said. "Hi, Pop! Look at *me*! I'm the first person ever to be sent by television!"

"Grab him!" ordered Mr. Wonka. "Quick!"

Mrs. Teavee shot out a hand and picked the tiny figure of Mike Teavee out of the screen.

"Hooray!" cried Mr. Wonka. "He's all in one piece! He's completely unharmed!"

"You call *that* unharmed?" snapped Mrs. Teavee, peering at the little speck of a boy who was now running to and fro across the palm of her hand, waving his pistols in the air.

He was certainly not more than an inch tall.

"He's *shrunk*!" said Mr. Teavee.

"Of course he's shrunk," said Mr. Wonka. "What did you expect?"

"This is terrible!" wailed Mrs. Teavee. "What *are* we going to do?"

And Mr. Teavee said, "We can't send him back to school like this! He'll get trodden on! He'll get squashed!"

"He won't be able to do *anything*!" cried Mrs. Teavee.

"Oh, yes I will!" squeaked the tiny voice of Mike Teavee. "I'll still be able to watch television!"

"*Never again!*" shouted Mr. Teavee. "I'm throwing the television set right out the window the moment we get home. I've had enough of television!"

When he heard this, Mike Teavee flew into a terrible tantrum. He started jumping up and down on the palm of his mother's hand, screaming and yelling and trying to bite her fingers. "I want to watch television!" he squeaked. "I want to watch television! I want to watch television! I want to watch television!"

"Here! Give him to me!" said Mr. Teavee, and he took the tiny boy and shoved him into the breast pocket of his jacket and stuffed a handkerchief on top. Squeals and yells came from inside the pocket, and the pocket shook as the furious little prisoner fought to get out.

"Oh, Mr. Wonka," wailed Mrs. Teavee, "how can we make him grow?"

"Well," said Mr. Wonka, stroking his beard and gazing thoughtfully at the ceiling, "I must say that's a wee bit tricky. But small boys are extremely springy and elastic. They stretch like mad. So what we'll do, we'll put him in a special machine I have for testing the stretchiness of chewing-gum! Maybe that will bring him back to what he was."

"Oh, thank you!" said Mrs. Teavee.

"Don't mention it, dear lady."

"How far d'you think he'll stretch?" asked Mr. Teavee.

"Maybe miles," said Mr. Wonka. "Who knows? But he's going to be awfully thin. Everything gets thinner when you stretch it."

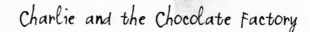

"You mean like chewing-gum?" asked Mr. Teavee.

"Exactly."

"How thin will he be?" asked Mrs. Teavee anxiously.

"I haven't the foggiest idea," said Mr. Wonka. "And it doesn't really matter, anyway, because we'll soon fatten him up again. All we'll have to do is give him a triple overdose of my wonderful Supervitamin Chocolate. Supervitamin Chocolate contains huge amounts of vitamin A and vitamin B. It also contains vitamin C, vitamin D, vitamin E, vitamin F, vitamin G, vitamin I, vitamin J, vitamin K, vitamin L, vitamin M, vitamin N, vitamin O, vitamin P, vitamin Q, vitamin R, vitamin T, vitamin U, vitamin V, vitamin W, vitamin X, vitamin Y, *and*, believe it or not, vitamin Z! The only two vitamins it doesn't have in it are vitamin S, because it makes you sick, and vitamin H, because it makes you grow horns on the top of your head, like a bull. But it *does* have in it a very small amount of the rarest and most magical vitamin of them all—vitamin Wonka."

"And what will *that* do to him?" asked Mr. Teavee anxiously.

"It'll make his toes grow out until they're as long as his fingers . . ."

"Oh, no!" cried Mrs. Teavee.

"Don't be silly," said Mr. Wonka. "It's most useful. He'll be able to play the piano with his feet."

"But Mr. Wonka . . ."

"No arguments, *please*!" said Mr. Wonka. He turned away and clicked his fingers three times in the air. An Oompa-Loompa appeared immediately and stood beside him. "Follow these orders," said Mr. Wonka, handing the Oompa-Loompa a piece of paper on which he had written full instructions. "And you'll find the boy in his father's pocket. Off you go! Good-bye, Mr. Teavee! Good-bye, Mrs. Teavee! And please don't look so worried! They all come out in the wash, you know; every one of them . . ."

At the end of the room, the Oompa-Loompas around the giant

camera were already beating their tiny drums and beginning to jog up and down to the rhythm.

"There they go again!" said Mr. Wonka. "I'm afraid you can't stop them singing."

Little Charlie caught Grandpa Joe's hand, and the two of them stood beside Mr. Wonka in the middle of the long bright room, listening to the Oompa-Loompas. And this is what they sang:

> *"The most important thing we've learned,*
> *So far as children are concerned,*
> *Is never, NEVER, NEVER let*
> *Them near your television set—*
> *Or better still, just don't install*
> *The idiotic thing at all.*
> *In almost every house we've been,*
> *We've watched them gaping at the screen.*
> *They loll and slop and lounge about,*
> *And stare until their eyes pop out.*
> *(Last week in someone's place we saw*
> *A dozen eyeballs on the floor.)*
> *They sit and stare and stare and sit*
> *Until they're hypnotized by it,*
> *Until they're absolutely drunk*
> *With all that shocking ghastly junk.*
> *Oh yes, we know it keeps them still,*
> *They don't climb out the window sill,*
> *They never fight or kick or punch,*
> *They leave you free to cook the lunch*
> *And wash the dishes in the sink—*
> *But did you ever stop to think,*
> *To wonder just exactly what*

Charlie and the Chocolate Factory

This does to your beloved tot?
IT ROTS THE SENSES IN THE HEAD!
IT KILLS IMAGINATION DEAD!
IT CLOGS AND CLUTTERS UP THE MIND!
IT MAKES A CHILD SO DULL AND BLIND
HE CAN NO LONGER UNDERSTAND
A FANTASY, A FAIRYLAND!
HIS BRAIN BECOMES AS SOFT AS CHEESE!
HIS POWERS OF THINKING RUST AND FREEZE!
HE CANNOT THINK–HE ONLY SEES!
'All right!' you'll cry. 'All right!' you'll say,
'But if we take the set away,
What shall we do to entertain
Our darling children! Please explain!'
We'll answer this by asking you,
'What used the darling ones to do?

Mike Teavee is Sent by Television

How used they keep themselves contented
Before this monster was invented?'
Have you forgotten? Don't you know?
We'll say it very loud and slow:
THEY . . . USED . . . TO . . . READ! They'd READ and READ,
AND READ and READ, and then proceed
TO READ some more. Great Scott! Gadzooks!
One half their lives was reading books!
The nursery shelves held books galore!
Books cluttered up the nursery floor!
And in the bedroom, by the bed,
More books were waiting to be read!
Such wondrous, fine, fantastic tales
Of dragons, gypsies, queens, and whales
And treasure isles, and distant shores
Where smugglers rowed with muffled oars,
And pirates wearing purple pants,
And sailing ships and elephants,
And cannibals crouching round the pot,
Stirring away at something hot.
(It smells so good, what can it be?
Good gracious, it's Penelope.)
The younger ones had Beatrix Potter
With Mr. Tod, the dirty rotter,
And Squirrel Nutkin, Pigling Bland,
And Mrs. Tiggy-Winkle and—
Just How The Camel Got His Hump,
And How The Monkey Lost His Rump,
And Mr. Toad, and bless my soul,
There's Mr. Rat and Mr. Mole—
Oh, books, what books they used to know,

Charlie and the Chocolate Factory

Those children living long ago!
So please, oh please, we beg, we pray,
Go throw your TV set away,
And in its place you can install
A lovely bookshelf on the wall.
Then fill the shelves with lots of books,
Ignoring all the dirty looks,
The screams and yells, the bites and kicks,
And children hitting you with sticks—
Fear not, because we promise you
That, in about a week or two
Of having nothing else to do,
They'll now begin to feel the need
Of having something good to read.
And once they start—oh boy, oh boy!
You watch the slowly growing joy
That fills their hearts. They'll grow so keen
They'll wonder what they'd ever seen
In that ridiculous machine,
That nauseating, foul, unclean,
Repulsive television screen!
And later, each and every kid
Will love you more for what you did.
P.S. Regarding Mike Teavee,
We very much regret that we
Shall simply have to wait and see
If we can get him back his height.
But if we can't—it serves him right."

CHAPTER TWENTY-EIGHT

Only Charlie Left

"Which room shall it be next?" said Mr. Wonka as he turned away and darted into the elevator. "Come on! Hurry up! We *must* get going! And how many children are there left now?"

Little Charlie looked at Grandpa Joe, and Grandpa Joe looked back at little Charlie.

"But Mr. Wonka," Grandpa Joe called after him, "there's . . . there's only Charlie left now."

Mr. Wonka swung round and stared at Charlie.

There was a silence. Charlie stood there holding tightly on to Grandpa Joe's hand.

"You mean you're the *only* one left?" Mr. Wonka said, pretending to be surprised.

"Why, yes," whispered Charlie. "Yes."

Mr. Wonka suddenly exploded with excitement. "But my *dear boy*," he cried out, "*that means you've won!*" He rushed out of the elevator and started shaking Charlie's hand so furiously it nearly came off. "Oh, I do congratulate you!" he cried. "I really do! I'm absolutely delighted! It couldn't be better! How wonderful this is! I had a hunch, you know, right from the beginning, that it was going to be you! Well *done*, Charlie, well *done*! This is terrific! Now the fun is really going to start! But we mustn't dilly! We mustn't dally! There's even less time to lose now than there was before! We have an *enormous* number of things to do before the day is out! Just think of the *arrangements* that have to be made! And the

people we have to fetch! But luckily for us, we have the great glass
elevator to speed things up! Jump in, my dear Charlie, jump in! You too,
Grandpa Joe, sir! No, no, *after* you! That's the way! Now then! This time *I*
shall choose the button we are going to press!" Mr. Wonka's bright
twinkling blue eyes rested for a moment on Charlie's face.

"Something crazy is going to happen now," Charlie thought. But he
wasn't frightened. He wasn't even nervous. He was just terrifically
excited. And so was Grandpa Joe. The old man's face was shining with
excitement as he watched every move that Mr. Wonka made. Mr. Wonka
was reaching for a button high up on the glass ceiling of the elevator.
Charlie and Grandpa Joe both craned their necks to read what it said on
the little label beside the button.

It said . . . UP AND OUT.

"*Up* and *out*," thought Charlie. "What sort of a room is that?"

Mr. Wonka pressed the button.

The glass doors closed.

"Hold on!" cried Mr. Wonka.

Then *WHAM!* The elevator shot straight up like a rocket! "Yippee!" shouted Grandpa Joe. Charlie was clinging to Grandpa Joe's legs and Mr. Wonka was holding on to a strap from the ceiling, and up they went, up, up, up, straight up this time, with no twistings or turnings, and Charlie could hear the whistling of the air outside as the elevator went faster and faster. "Yippee!" shouted Grandpa Joe again. "Yippee! Here we go!"

"Faster!" cried Mr. Wonka, banging the wall of the elevator with his hand. "Faster! Faster! If we don't go any faster than this, we shall never get through!"

"Through what?" shouted Grandpa Joe. "What have we got to get through?"

"Ah-ha!" cried Mr. Wonka. "You wait and see! I've been *longing* to press this button for years! But I've never done it until now! I was tempted many times! Oh, yes, I was tempted! But I couldn't bear the thought of making a great big hole in the roof of the factory! Here we go, boys! Up and out!"

"But you don't mean . . ." shouted Grandpa Joe. ". . . you don't *really* mean that this elevator . . ."

"Oh yes, I do!" answered Mr. Wonka. "You wait and see! Up and out!"

"But . . . but . . . but . . . it's made of glass!" shouted Grandpa Joe. "It'll break into a million pieces!"

"I suppose it might," said Mr. Wonka, cheerful as ever, "but it's pretty thick glass, all the same."

The elevator rushed on, going up and up and up, faster and faster and faster . . .

Then suddenly, *CRASH!*–and the most tremendous noise of splintering wood and broken tiles came from directly above their heads, and Grandpa Joe shouted, "Help! It's the end! We're done for!" and Mr. Wonka said, "No, we're not! We're through! We're out!" Sure enough, the elevator had shot right up through the roof of the factory and was now rising into the sky like a rocket, and the sunshine was pouring in through the glass roof. In five seconds they were a thousand feet up in the sky.

"The elevator's gone mad!" shouted Grandpa Joe.

"Have no fear, my dear sir," said Mr. Wonka calmly, and he pressed another button. The elevator stopped. It stopped and hung in mid-air, hovering like a helicopter, hovering over the factory and over the very town itself which lay spread out below them like a picture postcard! Looking down through the glass floor on which he was standing, Charlie could see the small far-away houses and the streets and the snow that lay thickly over everything. It was an eerie and frightening feeling to be standing on clear glass high up in the sky. It made you feel that you weren't standing on anything at all.

"Are we all right?" cried Grandpa Joe. "How does this thing stay up?"

"Sugar power!" said Mr. Wonka. "One million sugar power! Oh, look," he cried, pointing down, "there go the other children! They're returning home!"

CHAPTER TWENTY-NINE

The Other Children Go Home

"**W**e *must* go down and take a look at our little friends before we do anything else," said Mr. Wonka. He pressed a different button, and the elevator dropped lower, and soon it was hovering just above the entrance gates to the factory.

Looking down now, Charlie could see the children and their parents standing in a little group just inside the gates.

"I can only see three," he said. "Who's missing?"

"I expect it's Mike Teavee," Mr. Wonka said. "But he'll be coming along soon. Do you see the trucks?" Mr. Wonka pointed to a line of gigantic covered vans parked in a line nearby.

"Yes," Charlie said. "What are *they* for?"

"Don't you remember what it said on the Golden Tickets? Every child goes home with a lifetime's supply of sweets. There's one truckload for each of them, loaded to the brim. Ah-ha," Mr. Wonka went on, "there goes our friend Augustus Gloop! D'you see him? He's getting into the first truck with his mother and father!"

"You mean he's *really* all right?" asked Charlie, astonished. "Even after going up that awful pipe?"

"He's very much all right," said Mr. Wonka.

"He's changed!" said Grandpa Joe, peering down through the glass wall of the elevator. "He used to be fat! Now he's thin as a straw!"

"Of course he's changed," said Mr. Wonka, laughing. "He got squeezed in the pipe. Don't you remember? And look! There goes Miss Violet Beauregarde, the great gum-chewer! It seems as though they managed to de-juice her after all. I'm so glad. And how healthy she looks! Much better than before!"

"But she's purple in the face!" cried Grandpa Joe.

"So she is," said Mr. Wonka. "Ah, well, there's nothing we can do about that."

"Good gracious!" cried Charlie. "Look at poor Veruca Salt and Mr. Salt and Mrs. Salt! They're simply *covered* with garbage!"

"And here comes Mike Teavee!" said Grandpa Joe. "Good heavens! What have they done to him? He's about ten feet tall and thin as a wire!"

"They've overstretched him on the gum-stretching machine," said Mr. Wonka. "How very careless."

"But how dreadful for him!" cried Charlie.

"Nonsense," said Mr. Wonka, "he's very lucky. Every basketball team in the country will be trying to get him. But now," he added, "it is time we left these four silly children. I have something very important to talk to you about, my dear Charlie." Mr. Wonka pressed another button, and the elevator swung upward into the sky.

CHAPTER THIRTY

Charlie's Chocolate Factory

The great glass elevator was now hovering high over the town. Inside the elevator stood Mr. Wonka, Grandpa Joe, and little Charlie.

"How I love my chocolate factory," said Mr. Wonka, gazing down. Then he paused, and he turned around and looked at Charlie with a most serious expression on his face. "Do *you* love it too, Charlie?" he asked.

"Oh, yes," cried Charlie, "I think it's the most wonderful place in the whole world!"

"I am very pleased to hear you say that," said Mr. Wonka, looking more serious than ever. He went on staring at Charlie. "Yes," he said, "I am very pleased indeed to hear you say that. And now I shall tell you why." Mr. Wonka cocked his head to one side and all at once the tiny twinkling wrinkles of a smile appeared around the corners of his eyes, and he said, "You see, my dear boy, I have decided to make you a present of the whole place. As soon as you are old enough to run it, the entire factory will become yours."

Charlie stared at Mr. Wonka. Grandpa Joe opened his mouth to speak, but no words came out.

"It's quite true," Mr. Wonka said, smiling broadly now. "I really am giving it to you. That's all right, isn't it?"

"*Giving* it to him?" gasped Grandpa Joe. "You must be joking."

"I'm not joking, sir. I'm deadly serious."

"But . . . but . . . why should you want to give your factory to little Charlie?"

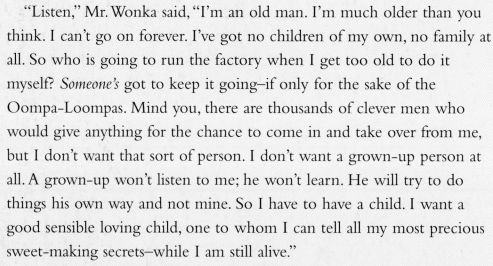

"Listen," Mr. Wonka said, "I'm an old man. I'm much older than you think. I can't go on forever. I've got no children of my own, no family at all. So who is going to run the factory when I get too old to do it myself? *Someone's* got to keep it going—if only for the sake of the Oompa-Loompas. Mind you, there are thousands of clever men who would give anything for the chance to come in and take over from me, but I don't want that sort of person. I don't want a grown-up person at all. A grown-up won't listen to me; he won't learn. He will try to do things his own way and not mine. So I have to have a child. I want a good sensible loving child, one to whom I can tell all my most precious sweet-making secrets—while I am still alive."

"*So that* is why you sent out the Golden Tickets!" cried Charlie.

"Exactly!" said Mr. Wonka. "I decided to invite five children to the factory, and the one I liked best at the end of the day would be the winner!"

"But Mr. Wonka," stammered Grandpa Joe, "do you really and truly mean that you are giving the whole of this enormous factory to little Charlie? After all . . ."

"There's no time for arguments!" cried Mr. Wonka. "We must go at once and fetch the rest of the family—Charlie's father and his mother and anyone else that's around! They can all live in the factory from now on! They can all help to run it until Charlie is old enough to do it by himself! Where do you live, Charlie?"

Charlie peered down through the glass floor at the snow-covered houses that lay below. "It's over there," he said, pointing. "It's that little cottage right on the edge of the town, the tiny little one . . ."

"I see it!" cried Mr. Wonka, and he pressed some more buttons and the elevator shot down toward Charlie's house.

"I'm afraid my mother won't come with us," Charlie said sadly.

"Why ever not?"

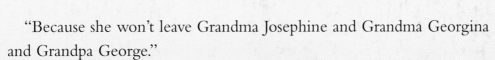

"Because she won't leave Grandma Josephine and Grandma Georgina and Grandpa George."

"But they must come too."

"They can't," Charlie said. "They're very old and they haven't been out of bed for twenty years."

"Then we'll take the bed along as well, with them in it," said Mr. Wonka. "There's plenty of room in this elevator for a bed."

"You couldn't get the bed out of the house," said Grandpa Joe. "It won't go through the door."

"You mustn't despair!" cried Mr. Wonka. "Nothing is impossible! You watch!"

The elevator was now hovering over the roof of the Buckets' little house.

"What are you going to do?" cried Charlie.

"I'm going right on in to fetch them," said Mr. Wonka.

"How?" asked Grandpa Joe.

"Through the roof," said Mr. Wonka, pressing another button.

"No!" shouted Charlie.

"Stop!" shouted Grandpa Joe.

CRASH went the elevator, right down through the roof of the house into the old people's bedroom. Showers of dust and broken tiles and bits of wood and cockroaches and spiders and bricks and cement went raining down on the three old ones who were lying in bed, and each of them thought that the end of the world was come. Grandma Georgina fainted, Grandma Josephine dropped her false teeth, Grandpa George put his head under the blanket, and Mr. and Mrs. Bucket came rushing in from the next room.

"Save us!" cried Grandma Josephine.

"Calm yourself, my darling wife," said Grandpa Joe, stepping out of the elevator. "It's only us."

"Mother!" cried Charlie, rushing into Mrs. Bucket's arms. "Mother! Mother! Listen to what's happened! We're all going back to live in Mr. Wonka's factory and we're going to help him to run it and he's given it *all* to me and . . . and . . . and . . . and . . ."

"What *are* you talking about?" said Mrs. Bucket.

"Just look at our house!" cried poor Mr. Bucket. "It's in ruins!"

"My dear sir," said Mr. Wonka, jumping forward and shaking Mr. Bucket warmly by the hand, "I'm so very glad to meet you. You mustn't worry about your house. From now on, you're never going to need it again, anyway."

"Who *is* this crazy man?" screamed Grandma Josephine. "He could have killed us all."

"This," said Grandpa Joe, "is Mr. Willy Wonka himself."

It took quite a time for Grandpa Joe and Charlie to explain to everyone exactly what had been happening to them all day. And even then they all refused to ride back to the factory in the elevator.

"I'd rather die in my bed!" shouted Grandma Josephine.

"So would I!" cried Grandma Georgina.

"I refuse to go!" announced Grandpa George.

So Mr. Wonka and Grandpa Joe and Charlie, taking no notice of their screams, simply pushed the bed into the elevator. They pushed Mr. and Mrs. Bucket in after it. Then they got in themselves. Mr. Wonka pressed a button. The doors closed. Grandma Georgina screamed. And the elevator rose up off the floor and shot through the hole in the roof, out into the open sky.

Charlie climbed on to the bed and tried to calm the three old people who were still petrified with fear. "Please don't be frightened," he said. "It's quite safe. And we're going to the most wonderful place in the world!"

"Charlie's right," said Grandpa Joe.

"Will there be anything to eat when we get there?" asked Grandma Josephine. "I'm starving! The whole family is starving!"

"Anything to *eat*?" cried Charlie, laughing. "Oh, you just wait and see!"

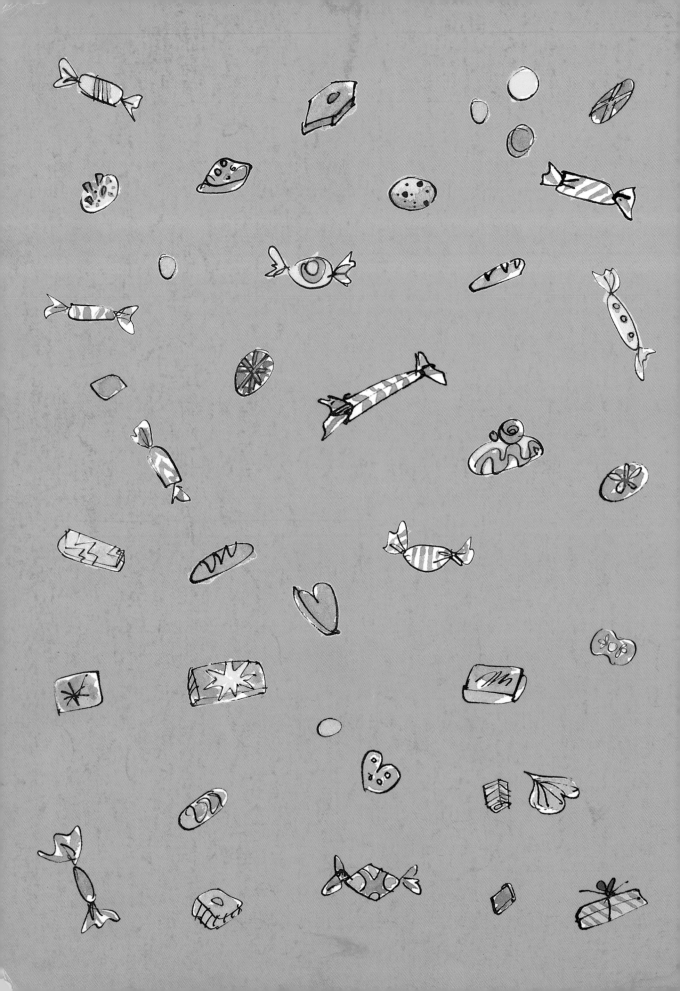

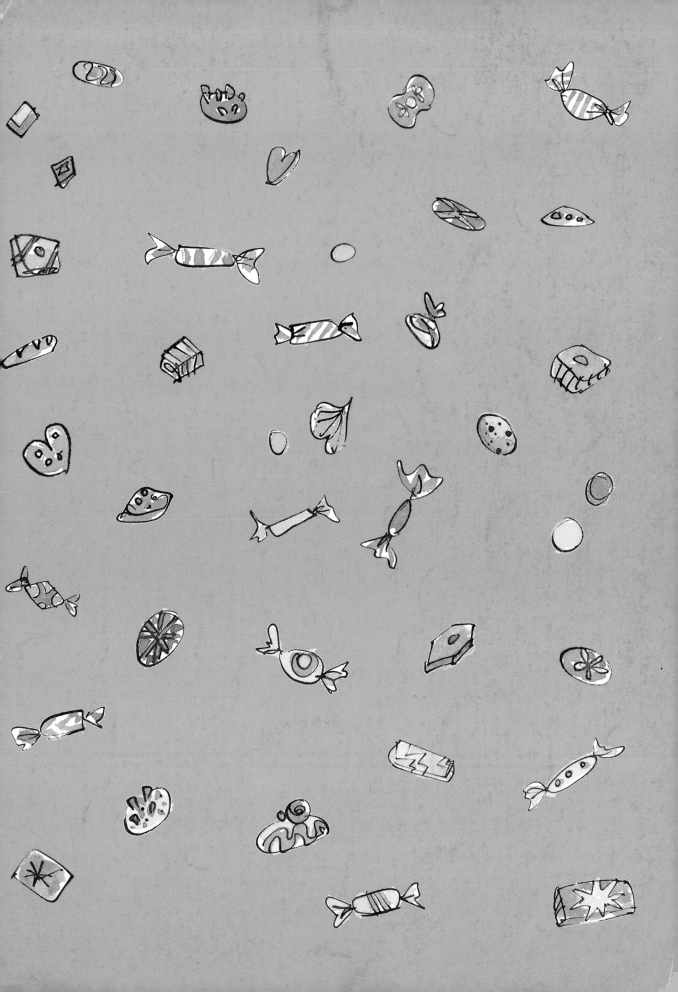

A STEP-BY-STEP BOOK ABOUT
IGUANAS

JACK HARRIS

ACKNOWLEDGMENTS

The author would like to thank the following persons for their help in the preparation of this volume: the staff and personnel of the Cattus Island Environmental Center, Ocean County Park & Recreation Department, Toms River, New Jersey; Ms. Paula Rosser of the Neptune Animal Hospital, Neptune, New Jersey; and Ms. Dot Steinberg, 88 Pet World, Bricktown, New Jersey.

DEDICATION
To my best friend
David
who taught me some fascinating things
about reptiles and amphibians.

Photographers: Glen S. Axelrod, Dr. Herbert R. Axelrod, Horst Bielfeld, Isabelle Francais, Michael Gilroy, Hilmar Hansen, Jack Harris, Ken Lucas (Steinhart Aquarium), S. Minton, K.T. Nemuras, Elaine Radford, Robert S. Simmons, Tidbits Studio.

Humorous drawings by Andrew Prendimano.

1995 Edition

Distributed in the UNITED STATES to the Pet Trade by T.F.H. Publications, Inc., One T.F.H. Plaza, Neptune City, NJ 07753; distributed in the UNITED STATES to the Bookstore and Library Trade by National Book Network, Inc. 4720 Boston Way, Lanham MD 20706; in CANADA to the Pet Trade by H & L Pet Supplies Inc., 27 Kingston Crescent, Kitchener, Ontario N2B 2T6; Rolf C. Hagen Ltd., 3225 Sartelon Street, Montreal 382 Quebec; in CANADA to the Book Trade by Vanwell Publishing Ltd., 1 Northrup Crescent, St. Catharines, Ontario L2M 6P5 ; in ENGLAND by T.F.H. Publications, PO Box 15, Waterlooville PO7 6BQ; in AUSTRALIA AND THE SOUTH PACIFIC by T.F.H. (Australia), Pty. Ltd., Box 149, Brookvale 2100 N.S.W., Australia; in NEW ZEALAND by Brooklands Aquarium Ltd. 5 McGiven Drive, New Plymouth, RD1 New Zealand; in Japan by T.F.H. Publications, Japan—Jiro Tsuda, 10-12-3 Ohjidai, Sakura, Chiba 285, Japan; in SOUTH AFRICA by Lopis (Pty) Ltd., P.O. Box 39127, Booysens, 2016, Johannesburg, South Africa. Published by T.F.H. Publications, Inc.
MANUFACTURED IN THE UNITED STATES OF AMERICA
BY T.F.H. PUBLICATIONS, INC.

CONTENTS

INTRODUCTION

During the 1950s, the drive-in movie theaters around the United States would attract thousands of teenagers with fantastic adventures involving prehistoric beasts. Because of some amazing atomic accident or by being thawed out after eons in suspended animation, these beasts would return from out of the past and attack mankind, leveling cities from New York to Tokyo.

Many of the human actors of these epics went on to become respected stars in more legitimate films. The real stars, however, the "dinosaurs" themselves, were often totally over-looked. What were these "monsters" that thrilled a generation of movie-goers? Many of these creatures were simply iguanas and other large lizards wearing make-up and photographed at extreme close-up to simulate the gigantic size of their prehistoric ancestors.

While the vast majority of these films of the 50s are easily forgettable, they do illustrate the continual fascination people have regarding iguanas and similar lizards. Their resemblance to the dinosaurs of prehistoric times and to the dragons in the legends of many cultures of both East and West has assured the iguana a unique place in animal history.

Tracing the origin of the idea of keeping an iguana as a pet is an impossible task. There is no record of when the first AmerIndians began keeping and caring for the iguana as a companion rather than keeping one around as a potential meal. Equally hard to pin down is the *reason* someone might desire to house such a creature as a pet. Even iguana owners themselves are hard pressed to explain the basis of their awe of these often mysterious miniature "monsters."

Opposite: Resembling miniature dinosaurs, iguanas are fascinating creatures that continue to gain new fans.

One of the most popular pet lizards is the common green iguana, *Iguana iguana,* probably the largest lizard in the Americas. The green iguana is actually part of a much larger group of lizards called the iguanids that include such diverse types as horned "toads," anoles or American chameleons, collared lizards, and Galapagos marine iguanas. They are found mostly in the New World, except for some species on the South Pacific islands and Madagascar. These lizards belong to the family Iguanidae.

WHAT IS AN IGUANA?

The agamid lizards of Australasia, Africa, and Eurasia are very similar to iguanids and seem to replace them in almost all the Old World. They belong to the family Agamidae.

Being strictly a New World species, green iguanas weren't known to Western culture until the European explorers of America began to keep journals and write letters referring to their discoveries. Animals held only a passing interest to explorers interested in gold and conquest, so it was many years before any real scientific study of iguanas (or any New World animals) was conducted. The first known specific reference to iguanas was in a work entitled *Decades* by Eden, which stated, in part, "Foure footed beastes . . . named Iuanna, muche lyke unto Crocodiles of eight foot length, of moste pleasunte taste."

The name iguana has had various spellings through the centuries including *iuanna, iwana, iguano, yguana, guana, wana, gwane, gwayn, yuana, igoana,* and *hiuana.* Some references trace the name *iguana* to the Carib Indian name for the

Opposite: The common green iguana is a member of the family Iguanidae. Other members of this family include horned toads, anoles, collared lizards, and Galapagos marine iguanas.

6

animals. These Indians still inhabit the coasts of Guiana, Venezuela, Dominica, Honduras, Guatemala, and Nicaragua, all regions where iguanas may be found. The name is derived from the Spanish equivalent of the Carib name, *iwana*. The common iguana was scientifically described and named by Linnaeus in 1758, while its very similar Caribbean relative, *Iguana delicatissima*, was named by Laurenti in 1768; thus both true iguanas have been known formally by Latin names for over 200 years.

Most experts agree that, while there are only about a dozen "real iguanas," many similar-looking lizards are often referred to as "iguanas." For our purposes we will consider mainly *Iguana iguana*, as the other "real iguanas" are virtually never for sale—many are on the endangered species list. Other "real iguanas" include species of *Cyclura*, the rhinoceros iguanas; *Amblyrhynchus* and *Conolophus*, the Galapagos iguanas; *Brachylophus*, the Fiji iguanas; *Ctenosaura*, the occasionally available spiny-tailed iguanas; and *Dipsosaurus*, the desert iguana. Because of their size, basilisks *(Basiliscus)* and chuckwallas *(Sauromalus)* are often considered "pseudoiguanas."

The banded basilisk, *Basilicus vittatus*, is sometimes mistakenly referred to as an iguana.

What is an Iguana?

Three genera of much smaller lizards that look a bit like young iguanas are also sometimes called iguanas—*Laemanctus* (cone-headed lizards), *Corytophanes* (helmeted or forest iguanas), and *Enyaliosaurus* (girdle-tail iguanas).

The only really common iguana is the green iguana *(Iguana iguana).* Its natural habitat extends from the lowlands of central Mexico into the southern tip of South America. It is usually found near ponds and rivers at altitudes from sea level to the mountains. Since these iguanas like to spend their days basking on the branches of trees that hang out over a body of water, they are also often called tree iguanas. This seems quite appropriate since, for all intents and purposes, they are more arboreal than terrestrial. They appear to enjoy their high tree positions for protection since at the first sign of any danger they can drop into the water below. They are able to remain submerged sometimes as long as half an hour, emerging at a different location when they feel that danger has passed. They have also been known to drop to the ground with a loud crashing noise that helps frighten potential attackers. The adults take the loftier positions, the young staying closer to the ground. A large tree can often house a dozen or more adult iguanas. In the rainy season, many behavioral scientists report that it is easier to find an iguana on the ground.

Green iguanas are very good swimmers and are excellent at running, climbing, and diving as well. The iguana is considered a delicacy in many regions and has been hunted almost to extinction. It is said that the taste of iguana tail (the most popular part) is similar to roast chicken. They are known in many parts of Latin America as *gallina de palo,* or chicken of the tree. In areas where iguanas are still plentiful, young boys will follow a river until they find a gathering of iguanas. One of the boys will climb the tree and frighten them. As is their nature, the animals will drop from their high perches into the water and attempt to escape. Ready for them, the other boys in the group will dive into the water and quickly capture them. The animals will try to hide amid the rocks at the bottom of the water, but the boys know these hiding places and the animals are caught. The boys are efficient, one of the reasons why the animals are becoming scarce in certain areas.

In areas where protective laws have been passed, the wild iguana populations seem to be increasing.

After they are sold to local merchants, who in turn sell them to the public, they are often displayed alive suspended by the tendons of their hind legs in a ghastly, inhumane fashion. Where laws have been enacted to protect the animals, their numbers in the wild appear to be increasing. They are considered a highly valuable food source, and studies continue toward the creation of iguana ranches and farms expressly designed to supply food.

Young green iguanas hatch in May, measure approximately eight inches in length at birth, and are colored a bright green. As they reach maturity, this bright color fades to a dull gray-green with a tinge of blue on the head. All iguanas have large, flexible spines beginning at the nape of their neck and extending down the entire body length, ending at the tip of the tail. This row of spines is higher in the males. The difference in spine size is only noticeable in mature animals, since these are very small in young iguanas, regardless of sex. Iguanas have

large tuberculate scales below the posterior angle on the jaw, with one scale being very much larger than the others and rounded.

Iguanas have short, thick tongues that are slightly notched instead of the long, forked tongues possessed by some other lizards and the snakes. They have round-pupiled eyes with well-developed lids.

The iguana's climbing ability is made possible by its strong legs, long toes, and heavy claws. The second and third toes of its five-toed foot are much longer than the others, allowing it a firm and strong grip.

The tail of the green iguana can be regenerated, a characteristic common to many members of the family Iguanidae. The animal can drop its tail if seized from behind by an enemy. The tail will continue to move for a time, keeping the attacker's attention while the iguana flees to safety. Although the tail will grow back, its color will be slightly different from the original tail and the break-line will be easily seen. The tail is often longer than the animal's trunk, making up well over half of its overall length of almost six feet.

Iguanas employ their tails as weapons, thrashing them about like a whip to fend off enemies. The scales of the crest on the tail resemble the teeth of a saw and, when swung at sufficient speed, can actually cut through cloth. Some larger iguanas have been observed knocking dogs out of action with the fast movement of their muscular tails. They have a natural fear of dogs and dog-like animals.

The green color and subdued pattern help them hide from enemies. An iguana's ability to remain almost completely motionless is also utilized to protect it in the wild.

Hanging down from the iguana's chin is a large flap of skin, the dewlap or throat fan. The size depends on the overall size of the animal. The larger the animal, the larger this flap of skin appears. As with the spines, the dewlap is larger in the males than females. The males use their dewlap to show off to the females and to ward off other males. They can erect the dewlap to increase their apparent size when viewed from the side or front, increasing their attractiveness to a female or their scariness to a rival. Males employ this trick to establish their

territory without actually having to fight rivals. Often a male will simply open its mouth in order to frighten off enemies.

If fighting does occur, the males will spread their dewlaps and raise their bodies up on all fours. They curve their backs and turn their compressed bodies in the direction of their enemy. If this challenge is met, the two iguanas will circle one another and, facing each other head-on, will thrash their heads together until one is defeated and departs. If the one iguana does not want to challenge the other, it will assume a submissive position by pressing itself firmly onto the ground.

Iguanas usually do not make any sounds. However, if the animal feels that it is cornered or trapped, it is able to utter a guttural hissing sound to frighten what it sees as potential attackers or threats.

Female iguanas are not as aggressive as their male counterparts. Normally they only battle to protect their sleeping place from other female iguanas. In confined spaces there have been noted instances of females fighting for limited nesting areas.

Iguanas become sexually mature at between two to three years of age. During mating the male grasps the base of the female's tail with one hind leg while biting firmly on her neck or head. He sways his head back and forth during copulation, which lasts from one to 20 minutes. The female will store the sperm until she lays her eggs 49 to 90 days later. The female will begin existing almost exclusively on water about a week prior to laying her eggs. Then she will dig into wet sand and, over a period of about five hours, will lay a clutch of 20 to 30 eggs. The eggs are about 1½ inches long and ¾ inch in diameter.

Nesting time is the most aggressive time for the female, as she is extremely protective of her nesting space. She usually takes about two days to make her nest, which lies about a foot or a foot and a half from the surface. The burrow can often extend as much as six feet under the ground. After she has laid her eggs, she will fill the burrow with dirt and dead plant matter. After an average of about 16½ weeks the eggs will hatch and the young iguanas will dig up to the surface.

In the wild, the digging of the nest is often the only

A good way to tell an iguana's age is by looking at its color. Young iguanas are much brighter than adults.

time in the entire year that the female descends from her tree. It is quite possible for a male iguana to spend his entire adult life out on a limb.

It was not until 1984 that artificial incubation and hatching of iguana eggs was successfully developed. Success was noted by the Smithsonian Tropical Research Institute when they hatched 700 iguana eggs. However, this success was the result of research aimed at cultivating the animals as a food source rather than to increase the pet trade. Instances of successfully breeding pet iguanas are still rare.

In the drier coastal zones, behavioral scientists have noted that the iguana's growth follows an annual cycle. In the rainy seasons the adult iguanas store large quantities of fat in the angles of their lower jaws and in their neck regions. Food plant supplies decrease sharply at the beginning of the dry season and the adult iguanas experience a marked weight loss during this time, being forced to live off their stored fat. They eat plants that they would ignore during the rainy season. The young iguanas still thrive on the insects found during this time.

Studies indicate that the animals in the wild have a high rate of reproduction and rapid growth. They have a life span of approximately ten years. There have been reports of iguanas living as long as 12 years in captivity.

Having prepared yourself to become the owner of a pet iguana by learning as much about the animal as you can, the next step is to actually obtain the animal. The best place to begin looking for the iguana you want is your local pet store. Pet store managers are the experts in all phases of caring for all kinds of pets.

SELECTING YOUR PET IGUANA

Some stores are more conventional, catering to dogs and cats or fishes. Others specialize in one type of animal, such as birds or hamsters, but they will probably be able to direct you to a shop that does carry iguanas. The best method is to begin your search with your phone book, calling the shops nearest you to see if they carry the kind of animal you want.

Since the iguana is still considered to be an "unusual" pet, you may have to contact quite a few stores before locating one that handles these reptiles. Even then, you may have to wait for a shipment to come in from the store's supplier. Iguana owners who have found the animals fascinating feel that the wait is well worth it.

Remember that you should not just go into a store and walk out with an iguana. You must also take into consideration the fact that you will have to buy all the necessary supplies to house, feed, and care for your pet. Calling ahead to make certain your local pet shop carries all the needed accessories is a wise plan of action. You must also remember these accessories when considering the price you're willing to pay for your new pet. Prices may vary widely, so shop around for the best price that you feel you can afford to pay for the pet and its accessories combined.

Opposite: It is a good idea to buy all necessary supplies before purchasing your pet (or pets).

Shops may also be willing to put you in touch with other iguana owners. Speaking and perhaps visiting these other owners would be an excellent educational experience prior to taking on the responsibility of iguana care yourself. Long-time owners will have met and often solved some of the problems and frustrations you may be about to face. Their advice, coupled with the expertise of your local pet shop proprietor, will help make you a better pet owner.

Observation is the key to making the final selection of your iguana. Once you have found a store that carries the animals, request a time to go and watch the animals before buying. There are certain important signs you should look for to assure yourself that you'll be taking home a healthy pet.

Pet shop managers are always concerned about the health of their stock. They will not sell a sick animal. They will appreciate it if you notice a symptom of oncoming disease in one of their animals. It will also show them that you're a knowledgeable shopper and will take good care of the animal you're planning to take home with you.

Watching an iguana is sometimes a lengthy task. Your potential pet should be active and vigorous. An alert iguana will flee at any quick movement such as the flick of a finger. An iguana that lies motionless on the bottom of its cage is probably suffering from a disease. An animal such as this should never be purchased.

However, if the iguana has been in the presence of people for a long time it may totally ignore humans and human attention, making it difficult to ascertain its general attitude. On the other hand, this lack of attention may give you the opportunity to observe other particulars that you should take into consideration when choosing which iguana will become your pet.

First of all, look at the animal's coloring. Since the common green iguana is the type you're most likely to find in your local pet store, the skin of younger specimens should be bright green in appearance (older animals often look more gray-green). If the animal shows a dull, yellowish skin, it is probably a sign of ill health. Similar to chameleons, iguanas can change color, but not as quickly or as radically. These color changes are

16

always in shades of yellow, moving to reds and greens. The iguana will shed its skin about four times during the year, the outer skin flaking off in small bits and pieces. This process appears to become accelerated after the animal has been submerged in water and its skin is drying out.

Examine the underside of its legs and the base of its tail. Healthy iguanas store fat in these areas, so the flesh should appear firm and full. This is also a good sign that the animal has

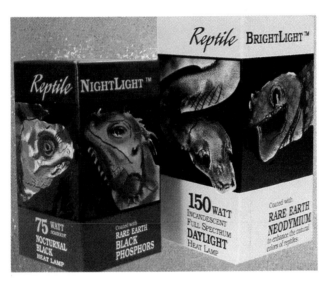

Some pet-product companies offer special bulbs that provide both light and heat for your reptile and amphibians. Such bulbs can either be found at or ordered through your local pet shop. Photo courtesy of Energy Savers.

been eating well. If these areas appear loose and flabby, there may be a dietary problem. Such problems may be easily eliminated with a diet change, but it's probably wise for such difficulties to be overcome by the pet shop rather than a new pet owner. The healthier the pet is when it's taken from the store, the healthier it will be when it moves into your home.

It is always a good idea to learn exactly what a healthy animal has been eating in the pet store. Continuing this diet when you bring the iguana home will help with the transition, allowing the animal to become used to its new environment in a shorter amount of time.

Profile of an iguana. The eyes of a healthy iguana should be clear and bright. Watery eyes are often signs of disease.

Take a good look at the animal's eyes. The round-pupiled eyes should be clear and bright and not watery. Watery eyes are one of the first signs of disease.

The flesh inside the iguana's mouth should be a healthy pink color. You can examine the animal's mouth by gently holding its upper jaw and carefully pulling down on the throat flap. Some iguanas develop sores or fungal growths in their mouths and have to be force-fed. Such infections show up as white and yellow spots in the mouth or as a cottony growth. These infections, often called "mouth rot," have proved very difficult to clear up.

Open sores around the nose and mouth area are normally caused by bad handling of the pet or they have been self-inflicted by the animal rubbing its nose against a wire cage. If you notice any such damage, avoid taking that particular iguana home.

There should also be no seepage of mucus or any fluid noted from the iguana's mouth or nose. These are bad signs, especially if you have other reptilian pets at home. They are usually symptoms of a respiratory infection that could prove fatal. An infected iguana could easily spread disease to other animals.

Examine the iguana's toes, claws, and tail. These should all be unbroken. Any injury, past or present, that is evident on the animal should be a reason not to choose that particular animal.

The younger and smaller the animal you take home, the more time you will have to enjoy it as a pet. Newly hatched iguanas are always hungry and will eat just about anything they are able to swallow. Older iguanas are more set in their ways and are more particular about what they eat. A new pet owner may want to consider obtaining a slightly older animal first, since such older animals have had the chance to change their diets more to vegetable matter than the insects preferred by younger iguanas. On the other hand, younger iguanas tend to be more adaptable to dietary changes. The advice of your pet store manager should be of great value in deciding on what age iguana would be best for you.

In general, regardless of age, iguanas are very adaptable to their surroundings. As long as you provide a comfortable temperature and the proper foods, keeping an iguana should not prove to be an overwhelming problem.

A healthy iguana will continue to grow for as long as it lives. Younger iguanas grow more rapidly than older ones since the whole growth process slows as the animals age. This must be remembered when you're planning on obtaining one as a pet. You must make certain you will be able to have the room needed for your animal both initially and in the future. Since they are tropical cold-blooded animals, they must be provided with a warm environment or they will not be able to properly digest their food.

Iguanas are extremely agile. They are very clean animals as well and can bend, twist, and turn to reach almost any area on their bodies to remove shedding skin or to scratch themselves. Some owners find it helpful to the animals to occa-

sionally clip their long claws.

There is no difference in the general attitude of the male or female iguana, so choosing one sex over another is not really a consideration when choosing one for a pet. Having two or more of the animals appears to present no particular problems. They tend to ignore one another for the most part, never sharing food whether it is provided or is caught (such as an insect).

Many of the iguanas sold in pet stores are already tamed. However, if you choose a younger one, you may have to tame it yourself. Some experts consider an iguana tame when it ceases to try to bite and quits thrashing its tail around in defense. If handled with care after training, the iguana will normally make no such threatening gestures. The longer it is cared for in captivity, the more docile it will become. Iguanas will depend on their human owners for food and care and will come to expect this particular kind of attention. Studies have shown that tame iguanas returned to the wild will quickly revert to their wild state. Despite this, within about a week initial taming will be accepted, and if the routines are continued, the animals will remain tame.

When initially dealing with a wild iguana, it is wise to wear some thick clothing, especially trousers to protect your legs from the whip-like action of the iguana's tail. This is their main line of defense when they feel cornered or threatened. If they are caught by their tail, they can drop it with only a drop or two of spilt blood (autotomy). The tail will regenerate at least partially after a couple of months. Have a black sack handy to place over the animal's head if it gets particularly unfriendly. Secured over its head, the sack will fool the iguana into thinking it is night and any frantic activity will cease. Additionally, it will protect you from the animal if it has a tendency to bite. An iguana bite will be very clean, but it should be disinfected immediately, as is the case with any animal bite. Tail lashings can leave a painful welt on an unprotected leg. Normally, these defenses are only put into play if the animal feels there is no escape. The iguana's first instinct against danger, real or imagined, is to run away or hide.

Some experts have reported success by making a cus-

Pet iguanas should receive a half-hour supervised exercise period each day.

tom harness for their iguanas with straps straddling the animal's forelegs and buckled across its back over its shoulders. Some cat harnesses can be easily adapted to this use depending on the size of your iguana. With the harness attached to something like a fishing line, you can let your iguana wander and exercise while keeping it in check. A half hour a day of this exercise is normally all it will need.

After this exercise period, hold the iguana's head with your index finger and forefinger positioned fork-like around its neck. Once secure, use the other hand to hold the iguana's chest with your palm and your fingers fork-like around the neck from underneath. Once you have the animal held in this fashion, you can hold it with the second hand alone and use a free finger to soothe its head gently. It will soon close its eyes.

Working with the animal for about an hour each day in this manner will render it tame in a week's time at most, possibly sooner.

Iguanas don't appear to enjoy being picked up often, preferring to climb on your shoulder if the surroundings are cool. They will stay in such lofty positions while you move about, but that is usually the extent of their desire to be "carried." If you must pick your pet up, do so by supporting its front legs and its abdomen. Iguanas won't use their claws to scratch you, since they appear to utilize their long toes and claws exclusively for climbing.

Since they are such clean animals, iguanas can be housebroken. If you maintain a regular feeding schedule, you

Untame iguanas tend to run away if they sense danger. If your new pet should get loose, go after him right away—an iguana is much faster than he looks.

The desert iguana, *Dipsosaurus dorsalis*, is rarely offered for sale. Unlike the green iguana, this reptile is basically a ground-dweller.

can usually predict when the animal needs to relieve itself. Their excrement resembles that of a chicken, depositing both solid and liquid wastes simultaneously. After depositing their waste, they will raise their tails and swivel their hips so they never touch their excrement. Since they will never deposit their waste in areas where they usually rest, it is no problem to provide a newspaper in a specific area at the specific time of day when the animals need it.

If you're looking for affection, don't choose an iguana for a pet. Iguanas will live with humans, but that is as far as it will go. A tame iguana may sit on your shoulder or lap, but only if your shoulder or lap is warmer than the surrounding room. A tame iguana will eat from your hand, but only if it is hungry at the particular time you're offering food. Don't be disappointed if it never nuzzles or cuddles up to you. It is just not in his nature.

The facts that they are unusual, quiet, and clean are the iguanas' most desirable traits. If these are the qualities that you desire in a pet, then the iguana is probably just the sort of animal to bring into your home.

If you have decided on purchasing an iguana to live in your home, you should always remember that its needs for survival may not match your own. Consideration of temperature and immediate environment must be made before making any kind of final decision regarding your new pet. Before you rush off to your local pet store, be certain that you are ready to make any necessary changes in your home to accommodate your pet iguana. Your pet shop proprietor can help you plan and prepare all the needed accessories. Consult with him or her before making your final selection.

HOUSING YOUR PET IGUANA

It is very common for an experienced pet owner to construct a good iguana home from simple and easy-to-get materials. For the beginner, readily available glass aquariums are probably the best bet. In recent years, a number of new versions of terrariums in space-age materials have been available on the market, and these are especially satisfactory.

After selecting the type of terrarium or aquarium you would like, you have to choose its specific shape and size. In the case of your iguana, the bigger, the better. Many people shop for pet cages as if they were shopping for a new piece of furniture rather than a home for their pet. It is true that you should look for something that fits in your home, both its decor and budget, but the needs of your future pet should certainly come first. If you feel that a large pet container will not fit into your home, then you should probably look for a different sort of pet.

Opposite: Be sure to consider the needs of the iguana when you begin to set up its terrarium. Tank size is of the utmost importance.

Your iguana will be happier if enough space is provided so it will not feel cramped or closed in. If iguanas experience this type of animal claustrophobia, they often refuse to eat and will actually die of starvation.

After determining the size of the terrarium or aquarium your house can accommodate, you should consider the shape of your pet's new home. Iguanas are, for the most part, tree animals. Taller cages will give you the best opportunity to set up the environment so your iguana can get up off the ground. By stocking the cage with pieces of driftwood or small trees, your animal will feel more at home right away. Add enough so that the animal can climb around since idleness can actually cause iguanas to become stiff and crippled. Sand smooth all such branches and fill in gaps so that mites will not have any breeding places. These branches should also be big enough for your iguana to rest comfortably on them. They should be arranged in such a manner that the animal can turn around on the branch, enabling it to come and go with ease. Iguanas enjoy basking in the heat and light and need such perches high from the floor of their homes.

Iguanas are arboreal—they live much of their lives in trees. Therefore, make sure your pet's tank contains branches for climbing.

Remember that in the wild iguanas like to lie in branches over a body of water. This gives them a feeling of security since they can drop into the water at any sign of danger. Arranging a piece of natural wood and a body of water in this fashion may be difficult in a homebound situation, but it is not impossible. With a shelf high over its terrarium or aquarium and a piece of rough, natural wood situated so your iguana can easily climb it, you could come close to simulating this natural environment.

In a short span of time an iguana will learn to climb up and down, going back and forth from its food and its toilet to the shelf to sit and digest its food.

Once the needs of the animal are met, it is easy to make your aquarium or terrarium into a beautiful addition to any decor. Real or artificial plants and rocks can make the animal's home functional, beautiful, and fascinating enough for both the animal and human observers to thoroughly enjoy. The advantage of utilizing artificial plants to decorate the terrarium is that the iguana won't eat them. Primarily vegetarians, they will eat just about any real plant you place within their reach. If you do have natural foliage, it is recommended that it be thick-leaved for minimal damage.

Real and artificial rocks are often used to form "caves" inside the aquarium or terrarium. As long as such structures are securely fastened down, they are fine. Be sure that there are no sharp edges or points on the rocks you use since, in the limited space of a cage, the chances for injury are greatly increased over the unlimited roaming space of the wild.

For smaller, younger iguanas about a foot in length, a cage 20 inches long by 12 inches wide should be adequate to keep the animal healthy. A full-grown six-foot iguana can be accommodated in a terrarium or aquarium measuring 60 inches by 60 inches by 30 inches if allowed the run of the house occasionally. This is, of course, the *minimum* size required. The more area your iguana has to explore, the more content it will be.

The bottom of the cage should be completely covered. Iguana keepers disagree on the best bottom coverings, but those often used include soil, gravel, sand, astroturf, and newspaper. Whichever you choose,

make sure your iguana cannot swallow the material. Feeding from a bowl will help ensure that this does not happen. Any iguana that eats large amounts of substrate *deliberately* has a dietary deficiency.

You should keep two containers on the floor of the cage, one for food and one for water. These containers should be at least an inch higher than the top layer of whatever material you've used to cover the bottom of the cage so the dirt, gravel, or sand cannot soil the containers' contents. You should also offer your pet some gravel, which it will ingest to help it digest its food. Simple trial and error will determine the size of gravel your iguana likes. Try a few sizes until you notice the animal ingesting a certain grade of gravel, then stick with that.

You should also provide another container of water large enough for your iguana to bathe in. The water temperature should be within the same range as the overall temperature of the aquarium or terrarium.

If you take the time to watch your animal's behavioral schedule, you'll be able to quickly determine when it likes to eat and when and where it prefers to deposit its waste. Once determined, you can provide newspapers at the proper time and place so your iguana will be, for all intents and purposes, "paper trained."

There are many methods of providing the necessary heat for your iguana's home. Since they are tropical animals, iguanas need moist heat for survival. Most iguana owners have achieved success in maintaining the proper temperature level by fastening an ordinary incandescent light bulb to the side or top of the cage. Some actually place it outside the cage, suspended near the top behind a wire screen. When a heat source is placed inside the cage, it must be separated from the animal with a protective wire covering. The iguana will constantly seek the source of heat and, if allowed to get too close, might burn itself on an exposed light bulb.

Some iguana keepers maintain the necessary temperature by running a small heating cable under a false plaster cage bottom, concealing it with the bottom materials. In the wild, iguanas follow the sun around for their needed warmth. This hidden cable method allows the keeper to landscape his or her terrarium, but it goes against the more natural methods that

Four Paws has made available a terrarium lining that is washable and mildew resistant. The lining's thick grass provides a healthy environment for small animals.

employ overhead heating.

Other keepers have reported success by immersing an aquarium heater with a thermostat in a water jar, allowing the cage to be heated by evaporating water. This also increases the humidity and prevents the water in your iguana's water dish from evaporating, which happens when utilizing any of the overhead heating methods. Be careful not to make your pet's environment too humid all the time. In the tropical homelands of iguanas, the heavy rainfall quickly evaporates, leaving the trees dry in a relatively short period of time. If an iguana's cage is humid for too long, it becomes a breeding ground for bacteria and fungi that can cause skin lesions and blisters.

Some pet owners provide their animals with heating pads. It is important to remember that the best judge of the proper heat for your pet iguana is the iguana itself. Never force

Iguanas are well known for their climbing activities. Don't be surprised to find your pet sitting on top of your favorite chair or sofa.

too much heat on the animal. If it becomes uncomfortable under a given heat source, it will simply move to a more pleasant location. Be certain you provide your iguana the means to move away from any given heat source whenever it wants.

Since in nature the temperature is never constant, it is not necessary to maintain a constant temperature for your animal. In the wild, the iguana thrives in temperatures ranging from 85° to 90°F during the daytime and 70° to 75°F at night. The animals require this heat to maintain proper digestion. If they are chilled after eating, their food may remain undigested in their stomachs, causing gas and perhaps even death.

It has become quite common among iguana owners to let the animals roam free in the house. As long as a regular feeding and watering area has been established, there are very few problems encountered. Be careful as to exactly in which parts of the house you allow your animal this freedom. The long claws on their toes can be hard on the furniture.

It is probably a good idea to warn visitors, *prior* to having them over, that they might encounter the creatures sitting on the backs of furniture or up on any of the higher points in rooms where they are able to climb. To calm your more excitable friends, you could use the custom harness method for your iguanas, adapting dog or cat harnesses, depending on the size of your iguana. With the harness you can walk your iguana while keeping it from wandering off on its own. Some iguana owners fasten such harnesses to themselves and let the iguana ride on their shoulders, making a unique and startling "decoration." Iguanas like to rest on human shoulders for warmth, especially if the surrounding room is cool.

Be careful not to let an untrained iguana escape into the outdoors. They are very speedy animals and are extremely difficult to catch. Being territorial in nature, they may not wander far, but they may still be hard to re-capture. This is true even indoors. When beginning your training routine, it will probably be a good idea to keep the animal within a confined area such as a small den or bathroom, just in case it tries to run away.

In warmer climates or in the warmer summer months in other areas, some pet owners may opt to construct an outdoor terrarium. With these constructions it is much easier to create a natural habitat for your pets. If you have any desire at all to try to breed your iguanas, the outdoor terrarium—a large one—is probably the best bet. Iguanas are extremely reluctant to breed in captivity. If they believe they are free (as would be the case in a large outdoor terrarium), they might be more comfortable in returning to their natural ways. Of course, a disadvantage of a large terrarium that simulates their natural habitat is that the animals may revert completely to their wild nature and any training they've received inside or in smaller quarters would probably be forgotten in six months or so.

Still, with the welfare of your pet in mind, a large outdoor terrarium is ideal in many situations. The varieties of outdoor terrariums are just as numerous as the ones for indoors. If constructing one on your own from brick or concrete, remember that the walls should be at least a yard high and protected in a way that will discourage invasion by rats, cats, dogs, and birds. Wire mesh over the top of the enclosure will serve this purpose as well as making it impossible for the iguanas inside to escape.

Of vital importance is the location of your outdoor terrarium. Adequate sunlight should strike the area so that your iguanas can enjoy sunning themselves at regular intervals. It should not be in a place where it receives direct sunlight all day. Adequate shade should be available naturally or by planting trees and shrubs within the enclosure.

The bottom of your outdoor terrarium should be covered with a layer of expanded clay or gravel with a layer of top soil, sand, or leaves on top of this. This will allow proper drainage. All of the accessories suggested for the indoor cages, such as perches, hiding rocks, etc., should be furnished in the outdoor terrarium as well. The structures should be as weatherproof as possible so they will last for longer periods of time.

While your pet store manager is the best person to question on the specific housing needs for your iguana, it would be valuable to be able to view practical housing arrangements that have already been established. If you know of an iguana owner or if your pet shop manager can introduce you to some, take an opportunity to view the pets in their homes.

Since 1952, Tropical Fish Hobbyist has been the source of accurate, up-to-the-minute, and fascinating information on every facet of the aquarium hobby. Join the more than 60,000 devoted readers worldwide who wouldn't miss a single issue.

Subscribe right now so you don't miss a single copy!

Four Paws Safety Screen Covers are designed to fit tanks of any size; they can be locked to ensure the safety of the pet.

These experienced owners will have faced any problems you may encounter and will be able to give good advice on how to overcome or prevent difficulties. Since they have a common interest with you, you could be establishing an ongoing relationship that will prove meaningful to you and your pet.

There are a number of theories regarding the exact diet of iguanas. The various ideas stem from a number of factors, including the species of the iguanas in question, their natural habitat, the time of year, and their general physical well-being.

FEEDING YOUR PET IGUANA

Iguanas in captivity have been observed enjoying completely different diets even though they might be similar in all other areas from age to sex to overall care. Some experts believe that the iguana instinctively eats the right kinds of food to give itself its own healthy, balanced diet. Others feel that the iguana will eat just about any variety of food and its complex digestive system will sort out and supply the animal with its specific needs.

Behavioral scientists who have worked with iguanas have established a few overall facts that pet owners can utilize to prepare the diet needed by their animals. In the wild, young iguanas have been observed eating insects, small rodents and birds, other small reptiles, snails, flowers and flower buds, and a variety of fruits and vegetables. As they grow older, this diet shifts over almost completely to vegetation.

To be certain of the continued health of your pet, you must supply an ample amount of the right kinds of food. With many other species of lizards, pet owners encounter problems finding the exotic foods these animals enjoy in the wild. Since the green iguana is almost always a complete vegetarian, obtaining its dietary needs is as easy as visiting your local supermarket. Younger green iguanas do like such things as grasshoppers, crickets, mealworms, earthworms, and even an occasional

Opposite: Young iguanas are insectivorous, while older ones are almost complete herbivores (plant eaters).

pinkie (just born) mouse. If your local pet shop does not supply such items directly, they will still be the people to go to to learn of a place where these specific iguana delicacies may be obtained.

In some areas these food animals are either difficult to obtain or expensive. Overcoming these obstacles means raising such food animals on your own. Your pet shop manager can probably help you begin to raise your own live food.

The first and most important rule of culturing any live food is cleanliness. This is true for the iguana's cage as well as the housing for the food animals. The breeding quarters for food animals should be dry and in a temperate room. Greenhouses with controlled temperatures or warm boiler rooms are often the ideal locations for such setups. A closet can be adapted easily for most of the living food young iguanas crave. Such closets should be insulated with tiles or foam sheets about an inch thick and illuminated with a fluorescent lamp. There usually is an additional incandescent bulb inside the food animals' individual breeding chambers. Openings near the top and bottom of the closet covered with wire mesh will provide even air flow for ventilation.

Crickets can be purchased at many pet shops, at bait shops, and through advertisements in various hobby journals. Once you have obtained a supply you will need a breeding box about 2 feet by 18 inches by 16 inches equipped with a light bulb for heat and a raised wire mesh floor. The box should be supplied with branches for climbing. The temperature should be kept at about 86-90°F with a relative humidity of 30%–40%. The crickets' food of bran, grasses, chopped fruit, lettuce, germinated wheat and similar items should be placed in a flat dish. Crickets like hiding places, so you can provide them with rolled up paper, newspapers, or stacked empty egg cartons.

In order to breed the adults, fill a four-inch flower pot to about three inches depth with moist sand and peat moss mixed together. Place the whole thing in a rearing container. After the crickets lay their eggs, the nymphs appear in about a week's time. They can be removed from the rearing container after about ten days and reach adult maturity after about seven weeks. Crickets should be dusted with vitamin supplements be-

fore being given to an iguana.

Mealworms can be found at many pet stores. To breed them for iguana food you will need a container 16 by 10 by 6 inches or something of comparable size with a fine wire gauze cover. This should be filled about halfway with wheat and crushed oats and covered with a newspaper. The temperature should be kept at about 80°F. The relative humidity should be 30%. Normal morning and evening lighting should be maintained. The food should be kept dry and can be supplemented

A proper diet is just as necessary for the iguana living in an outdoor environment as for an indoor pet. You cannot count on the outdoor iguana finding its own food.

by small chunks of carrots, apples, and other varieties of fruits and vegetables. This supplement should be replaced every other day so it does not go moldy. Do not allow any fungus growth to take hold in the container. After the eggs appear, the larvae will hatch in about six days, with the adult beetles reaching maturity in four to seven months.

There are a number of different fruits and vegetables that experts and pet owners have fed their iguanas with success. It would be an unusual animal that enjoyed all varieties

offered. The best way to find out what your animal enjoys is to offer a sampling of different kinds and take note of which it continually eats. All of these can be obtained in the local supermarket, but it would be best if you buy them from a fresh food stand or, better still, grow them yourself in your backyard.

Leafy items such as butter lettuce, head lettuce, romaine lettuce, celery tops, tomatoes, grated carrots, chard, and spinach are special favorites. (Many keepers believe lettuce to be poor in nutrients and to cause diarrhea. Use it sparingly.) Desirable fruits include most varieties of melons, bananas, apricots, and peaches. Drained canned fruits and fruit cocktail (a true iguana delicacy) are often substituted for fresh fruits when the latter are out of season. Iguanas will also accept such items as softened bread, cream of wheat, and mashed potatoes. Many iguanas thrive on flowers when in season, especially yellow flowers such as forsythia and dandelion.

Small amounts of cat or dog food can be added to the salad-like concoctions. This meat contains calcium, which the animals often need for good bone development and growth. These canned foods also contain a certain amount of salt, which the animals require. You will occasionally see liquid seeping from the animal's nostrils. This salty fluid is a normal elimination of bodily fluids, but it does indicate the animal's salt needs. Canned pet food helps replace this salt. If your animal is a *strict* vegetarian, it might be a good idea to sprinkle a *small* amount of table or sea salt on some of its vegetables. Vitamin supplements and edible bone meal should also be sprinkled on the food.

If you have purchased your pet from a pet shop, the owner will be able to tell you what kind of diet the animal has been enjoying. It is probably best to continue the same diet for a time after you bring the animal home. If you want to make a change, do so gradually so you can learn what other foods the animal will enjoy. There have been reports of some animals thriving on cheese and ice cream in a home environment.

Iguanas do not necessarily eat every day. Depending on their individual habits, they should be kept on a regular feeding schedule of at least three meals a week. You can determine your pet's schedule by simple observation, watching to

By giving lots of nutrients to your iguana's food items, you will then pass those nutrients on to your iguana. That's why it's a good idea to maintain those food items on specially formulated diets. Check your local pet store for such products. Photo courtesy of Fluker Farms.

see when it is interested in the food you give it. Once a few weeks go by, you should be able to tell exactly when the animal is hungry on a fairly regular basis. If your iguana is interested in eating every day, then feed it every day. Younger iguanas eat more often than the adults. When a younger iguana reaches a weight of about ten pounds, its interest in eating every day seems to wane. Iguanas adjust their own schedules. Do not try to force them to bend to your convenience.

Since the animal's digestion is greatly affected by the surrounding temperature, its eating habits will often reflect temperature changes. The higher the temperature, the more often your iguana will feed—it will eat more food more often. If you house your iguana in an area where it receives direct sunlight, it will generate its own vitamin D. Some owners have reported the successful use of an ultraviolet lamp to supply this need, as long as they restrict its use to 30-minute periods. If

sunlight is not readily available, some experts suggest using cod liver oil or a multivitamin prepared as an oil emulsion on the vegetables to supply the needed vitamin D.

If you live in an area of drastic temperature changes during the different seasons, then offer your iguana less food in the cooler winter months. The temperature range that is most comfortable for most iguanas is between 65°F and 85°F to 100°F. Your iguana's habits will be able to show you how to adjust both its feeding schedule and the temperatures it enjoys. If it appears sluggish because of the heat or cold, it will not eat properly.

Do not just put the food on the floor of the animal's cage. Use containers of easy-to-clean materials such as glass, metal, pottery, or plastic. These food containers should be at least an inch high and wide enough for the animal to actually climb inside. Iguanas enjoy digging and scratching around in their food before deciding exactly which item they are going to eat. Containers that are too small will not allow this habit to be practiced, and the animals could become frustrated. Once you have established a place for the containers, don't move them

Extruded foods provide captive reptiles with good nutrition and are easy to use; they also cause less mess. The Pretty Pets adult iguana food shown here comes in a resealable plastic bag to preserve freshness.

around. Iguanas are creatures of habit and expect their food to be in the same place all the time once it has been established. This is especially important with iguanas that are given free run of the house or have large areas in which to roam around. They *will* find it eventually if you move it, of course, but looking around might prove frustrating to the animal, and a frustrated iguana might not eat at all.

The Galapagos marine iguana *(Amblyrhynchus cristatus)* and the club-tail iguana *(Hoplocercus spinosus)* are both very difficult to keep alive in captivity. The marine iguana will not eat in captivity; the club-tail iguana eats mealworms and termites.

The desert iguana *(Dipsosaurus dorsalis)* is not an easy animal to keep in captivity either, since it requires a very high temperature to maintain its digestive abilities. It does, however, enjoy eating all parts of dandelions, lettuce, and the petals from geranium plants.

Common spiny-tailed iguanas *(Ctenosaura)* need more meat than green iguanas. Raw meat, small birds, rodents, insects, and raw eggs are some favorites of these species. The rhinocerous iguanas *(Cyclura)* like such things as berries and bananas added to their regular diet as well as mice and baby chicks, since they appear to need fur and feathers in their diets.

The Galapagos land iguana *(Conolophus subcristatus)* survives on a diet very similar to that of the common green iguana except for the fact that it needs additional salt. This is probably because of the sea spraying salt on its food in its natural habitat on the Galapagos Islands.

During certain times of the year you may note some fatty areas developing around the neck regions on the lower jaw of your animal. There is no need to worry about this. In the wild, iguanas will store fat in these areas in anticipation of drought periods when plants are scarce. They can actually live off this fatty tissue during these lean times.

For a long time it was believed that iguanas did not drink water. However, more and more behavioral scientists have observed occasional drinking by many varieties of iguana. Some have been seen lapping from pools while others have been observed tasting the dew from leaves. Whatever the case,

Some companies produce food cubes for iguanas with all the necessary nutrients already mixed in. All you really need to do is take one out of the container and present it to your pet. Photo courtesy of Ocean Nutrition.

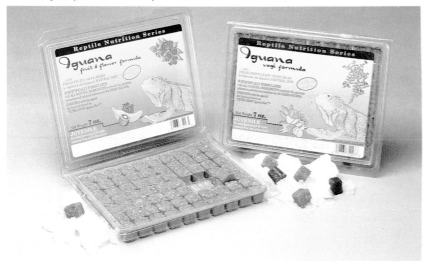

Lettuce may be a favorite of some iguanas, but it can cause diarrhea if too much is given. Therefore, feed it sparingly to your pet.

you must be certain that your animal always is provided with a water dish. This should be identical to the food dishes—an inch high and big enough for the iguana to climb into. Iguanas like to bathe and soak in their water. If a female iguana is about to lay a clutch of eggs, she will begin existing almost totally on water for about a week before she begins to lay. Some observers feel that their skin actually absorbs moisture, explaining the rarity of their drinking water directly. Make certain that the water dish is changed often so clean water is readily available. Bathing and soaking can quickly contaminate the water, and contaminated drinking water always presents dangers.

You should also supply your pet with some gravel. Iguanas ingest gravel to help their digestive system break down the tougher varieties of vegetable matter. Offer your pet a selection of different gravel grades at first to determine which kind it prefers. Avoid the fine varieties since they easily hold moisture and could cause mouth rot. Iguanas do not chew their food, gulping it down whole. The gravel helps grind the food into more easily digested pieces, much as happens in a chicken's gizzard.

Iguanas like to eat in peaceful and quiet surroundings. Recommended feeding times are the early morning and late evening. Leave your pet alone while it eats since it will not like to be disturbed during this time. If conditions are not exactly to its liking, the iguana will not eat.

The three-meals-a-week feeding schedule that many iguanas get used to makes leaving your pet alone for a day or two relatively easy. Leaving the animal on its own in a cage or in the house for any longer than this might present problems, since the water will not be changed and the waste areas will not be cleaned. If you must leave your animal for longer periods, it would be best to arrange for someone to come in and perform the simple duties of changing the water, providing fresh food, and cleaning the waste.

As long as you follow these simple guidelines about feeding your pet iguana, you should not encounter any unusual difficulties in maintaining a healthy and contented animal.

HANDLING IGUANAS

The exotic attractiveness of iguanas is one of the reasons most pet owners give for keeping one of these unusual animals. The facts that they are odorless, quiet, and do not require constant attention are other plus factors owners give when asked why they share their homes with such strange creatures.

The iguana is not recommended to those who want a pet for love and affection. Iguanas are not affectionate animals. In fact, they do not even like to be picked up and carried. If the surrounding room is cool, they will climb up and perch on your shoulder. This is not a display of affection toward you—it is due only to the fact that your body temperature is higher than that of the surrounding room. The iguana has come to you for warmth and nothing else.

Since iguanas are creatures of habit, they can be trained to accept food from your hand, but only if you offer the food at approximately the same time each day and under similar circumstances.

When you do find it necessary to pick up your animal, support its abdomen and its front legs. Due to their many double joints, iguanas are very agile. If they escape, they are quick and are difficult to recapture.

Never, under any circumstances, grab an iguana's tail. Like all members of the family Iguanidae, your iguana can detach its tail if it is seized from behind. The tail will grow back with time, but you should still strive to avoid grabbing it. Iguanas use their whip-like tails as weapons when frightened. The tail's serrated dorsal scales can cause some nasty welts or cuts.

Untamed iguanas can be aggressive if they believe you pose a threat to them. They don't often bite, but they will open their mouths and show their teeth in an effort to frighten any suspected enemy. In instances such as this you might hear the only noise iguanas ever make, a guttural hissing sound. If your

untamed animal does try to bite, place a black sack over the animal's head and its frantic activity will stop.

Iguanas don't use their claws for anything but climbing; they won't scratch you on purpose. However, some owners clip the claws so that an accidental scratch won't occur. Also, if you let your pet roam free over the furniture, clipped claws lessen the chances of a favorite piece of furniture being damaged by a climbing iguana.

If you handle your animal with continued care after it has become tame, threatening gestures with tail and teeth will cease. It will become more and more docile the longer it is in

Whenever you pick up your iguana, be sure to support its abdomen and its front legs. Never pick up an iguana by the tail.

your care. Some long-time iguana owners report that a few of their animals actually enjoy being rubbed on their heads since that is the one area of their bodies that they cannot reach despite their double joints. While it may appear to be an affectionate gesture, it is most likely one-sided.

If you have more than one iguana, you probably won't have any problems housing them together. They may have an initial confrontation, but they will soon establish their own territories and leave each other pretty much alone. If they are in close quarters they will probably tolerate each other up to the point where it appears that they are totally ignoring one another. They are not gregarious, even among their own kind.

IGUANA HEALTH

No matter how conscientious a pet owner you are, there is still the possibility that your animal will have to be treated for an injury or an illness. One of the positive aspects of owning an iguana is the fact that it is a hardy animal and resistant to most diseases. However, since there are some health problems iguana owners may encounter, you should be aware of them and the prescribed preventive measures. Also, a few of these diseases may present a slight danger to humans, so you have to know what signs are detectable.

While there are many specific symptoms for particular diseases, one of the best health barometers for iguanas is their overall color. Older iguanas lose the bright color of their youth, but the darker colors are still bright if the animal is healthy. If your mature animal seems to be losing color, it maybe the first indication of oncoming illness. If you notice such a dulling of the skin, begin a close watch of the animal's habits with regard to eating and its other normal routines. Any radical change may be cause for concern.

Parasites such as mites and ticks are probably the most common health threats iguana owners run across. These pests cause your pet considerable discomfort. If they are successfully removed from a young animal they will most likely never return. While they are small to minute creatures, many of these iguana parasites have complex and complicated life cycles. During some of these different stages the pests may leave the iguana altogether and seek another host. These new hosts may even be humans.

Iguana ticks resemble the common varieties that you see on dogs but are smaller. They are probably from the tropics and will not reappear once they are removed. The most successful method of removing these hard-to-see creatures is with the slow and steady tug of a pair of tweezers, making certain to get the head of the parasite. Some pet keepers recommend

Examine your pet iguana regularly for signs of ill health. Quickly noticing changes in the animal's routine may one day save its life.

smearing tobacco juice, lemon juice, alcohol, or vinegar on the tick, as they believe these might help force the parasites to release themselves more readily. Using tweezers to actually pull the pests off is still the only way to actually remove them. If these parasites are heavily dug in, it is wise to follow up their removal by swabbing the sore spot with alcohol. This will help to prevent possible future infection.

If your iguana seems irritated and its skin appears to be covered with a fine white dust, then it probably has mites. This white dust is made up from the mites' droppings. If you detect this, take steps to remove them as soon as possible. The mites are very small, so the white dust is probably the only way to know if they are present. A close look might reveal some of the tiny pests moving across the animal's neck or head. The head and neck area is also where you will probably see the largest concentration of white dust.

A healthy iguana will show no sign of seepage around the mouth or nose. Seepage is often a sign of respiratory illness.

Removal of mites requires soaking your iguana in warm water. While you have it immersed, scrub its cage thoroughly before replacing your pet. This single treatment will probably do the job, but be on the lookout since there may be mite eggs that will hatch later. If the mites do return, repeat the operation.

A homemade mite remedy can be made by mixing equal portions of 90% grain alcohol and castor oil. This mixture is brushed onto affected areas instead of immersing the animal. The grain alcohol is available at your local liquor or drug store. Common castor oil can also be found at any local pharmacy.

If both the homemade remedy and the bathing method fail to produce results, try dusting your iguana with Sulphanone, a mite poison that will not affect iguanas. Dri-Die 67 is a dehydrating agent that will remove all moisture from the tiny mites and destroy them. Like Sulphanone, the Dri-Die 67

can be dusted on your pet. After about 18 hours wash the powder off the animal with another warm water bath, rinsing often. The cage should also be dusted, but it should be thoroughly cleaned before returning the animal to its home. Both of these products are available from either your local pet store or your veterinarian. Check with them before using either of these products, however. Since the Dri-Die 67 removes moisture, too much may dry out a younger, smaller iguana along with the mites. This could prove fatal to your pet. Another danger may be present if the iguana inhales too much of these medications. Follow the recommendations of your pet shop owner or your veterinarian when using any drug or medication for *any* pet.

Your veterinarian will also have to be consulted if mites get into your pet's trachea and lungs after entering through the nostrils. These home remedies are effective only for parasites found on exposed areas of your iguana.

Your pet's home can be further protected from mites and ticks by hanging a one-inch square of common insecticide strip or a dog's flea collar inside the cage for three days. It also helps to make sure that these pests have no hiding places. Mites can hide in very small cracks. Prevention of parasite infestations is extremely important since many of these pests carry diseases that could lead to other illness in your pet.

Even if you feel you have totally solved the mite and tick problem, it is always best to give your iguana a weekly check for any recurrence of these parasites. Often ticks and mites lay eggs underneath the scales of the animals. It will take a few weeks for these to hatch and grow large enough to be detected.

Pin worms are one type of internal parasitic worm that may attack your iguana. If your animal loses weight even though it has been eating regularly, then such internal parasites may be the problem. Your veterinarian will discover the worms in the animal's cloaca and its feces and, if diagnosed in time, he will be able to cure your pet in most cases. The tragic fact is that most pet owners do not take their pets to the veterinarian for this problem until it is too late.

In any case of parasites, keep your animal isolated. Parasites can often be transferred easily from one animal to an-

other, and you then will have double the problem of administering medication.

Never use any form of DDT near your iguana or any pet reptiles. DDT, even in minute doses, is often fatal to reptiles.

Injuries to pet iguanas most often occur because of rough handling. The most common injury is the loss of the animal's tail. Since this is normal defense behavior, there is no need to be overly concerned if it happens. As the iguana's tail often makes up most of its overall length, owners may be shocked at how small the animal appears after dropping its tail. It will begin to regenerate after a few months, but it will never match its original color and the break point will be easily discernible.

If a tail break does occur, there will be a bloody stump where the tail used to be. This will heal quickly by itself, but you may want to apply an antiseptic to the stump to prevent any infection.

There are also instances when careless handling of iguanas results in broken toes or legs. If this happens, the best remedy is to keep the animal in peaceful surroundings and allow it to heal on its own. Sometimes claws are broken or actually pulled from their toes by being handled roughly. While you may want to prevent infection by applying an antiseptic to injured toes, don't expect the claws to regenerate. If any additional infection does set in, treat it with an antibiotic as recommended by your pet shop manager or your veterinarian.

Normally an iguana's claws will be slowly worn down by its daily climbing actions. Like human toenails, they will grow at a regular rate and replace themselves gradually. However, if you notice new claws coming in twisted, it might help your pet if you carefully trim them to shape. You can use a human nail clipper for younger animals and a dog claw clipper for older iguanas, since their claws tend to be harder. Be careful not to cut too close to the actual toe since there are nerves, veins and arteries connecting the nail near its base. Cutting into any of these will cause your animal injury and pain. If your iguana does start to bleed, you can apply antiseptic cream, but nature will usually take care of minor injuries such as these.

Iguana Health

If two iguanas engage in a physical battle, there maybe injuries in the form of open wounds or scratches. If they are left alone, they may heal with nature's touch, but there is a danger of the wounds becoming abscessed. Abscesses are often treated with an antibiotic injected with a hypodermic needle in-

Be sure that all branches placed in your iguana's environment are free from pesticides—especially DDT. If there is any doubt, leave it out!

tramuscularly. Pet owners are best advised to have their veterinarian handle this somewhat delicate chore. Your veterinarian might also suggest that you aid the build-up of antibiotics in your pet's system by supplementing the injections with oral antibiotics. You can also apply antiseptic directly to the wounds if it is an emergency and antibiotic treatment is not readily available.

Health problems might also arise if your animal is not fed properly. Even with the vegetable diets recommended, there still may be some required nutrition your animal is not receiving. Some keepers recommend a weekly dose of multivitamins mixed in the animal's food or given directly. These will give the animal the proper vitamins it would probably be obtaining for itself if it were existing in the wild. Proper intake of

these essentials will better prepare the animal's system for combat against illness and injury. Exact dosages for multivitamins depend on the variety you adminster to your pet. Your local pet shop may have such vitamins specifically for lizards and iguanas. If so, follow the directions on the containers. Your pet shop manager may also suggest the use of bird vitamins. Children's vitamins can also be used for iguanas, though they are not the best. Whatever supplement you use, be sure to follow manufacturer's instructions.

At first you may feel that vitamin supplements may not be necessary. However, since the animals are in captivity they do not have the opportunity to naturally seek out the vitamins they need. Lack of certain important vitamins can be extremely dangerous to your animals. For instance, a lack of vitamin D will prevent the animal from receiving any nutritional benefit from the minute amounts of calcium it does receive. Direct sunlight or light from a fluorescent lamp designed for use with reptiles will enable the iguana to produce its own vitamin D naturally. The animal must be exposed to this light directly, not through the glass of its cage since the glass will filter out the radiation necessary for the production of vitamin D.

If your iguana is not receiving enough calcium, its bones could eventually become soft and develop improperly. Deformities of this nature could prove fatal after a time. To prevent this, widen the range of your pet's diet. This precaution is especially important with the younger iguanas since they are experiencing the most rapid growth. If any exhausted animal does not appear to be gaining energy from a broader diet, take it to your veterinarian. He might recommend an injection of calcium gluconate if the animal is suffering from acute fatigue.

Once your pet begins to respond to the change in diet, supplement its food intake with extra vitamin D by slightly oiling it with irradiated cod liver oil and also dust the food with powdered calcium. After recovery seems to be complete, maintain the new diet, variety and all, and continue regular calcium supplements. With younger iguanas, provide the most varied diet possible, including such things as high-quality canned dog food, dandelion flowers, roses, and whole small mice to supplement the dusted mealworms and crickets.

Iguana Health

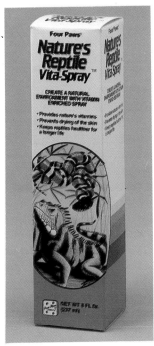

Nature's Reptile Vita-Spray by Four Paws was formulated by veterinarians and herpetologists and contains essential vitamins that are important for reptiles' health.

Remember that temperature control is vitally important in keeping iguanas. A danger of subjecting your animal to cool drafts and low temperatures is the possibility of lung infections. These are actually caused by bacteria, but the lower temperatures increase the chances of the bacteria surviving and the animal becoming susceptible. If this happens to your pet, you will notice it having difficulty in breathing; in addition, there may be a foamy discharge from the mouth. Heat and an antibiotic will probably cure your pet if you follow your veterinarian's advice on the proper dosage.

A digestive tract infection is probably the problem if your pet is regurgitating partially digested food. This and a refusal to eat are common symptoms of this disorder. Since iguanas sometimes wait three days between meals, it may be difficult to determine if they are eating or not. If you have been

following a prescribed schedule, you should notice any actual change in the routine on the animal's part within a week's time. Digestive tract problems are usually caused by bacteria.

Mouth rot is an extremely dangerous problem for iguanas. While not fatal in itself, it prevents the animals from eating and they will eventually starve to death. It appears as yellow patches and crusts and a cottony collection of matter on the animal's gums and jaws. It is an infectious bacterial disease and usually occurs after an injury in an animal with a vitamin deficiency. Such injuries may be the result of a fight with another iguana or of simply rubbing up against the sides of the cage. Penicillin ointment applied to the infected areas is one remedy, and other antibiotics may prove effective as well. They should be applied once a day until the condition has completely cleared up. Your veterinarian may want to inject these into your pet. Since most antibiotics are available only through your veterinarian, it's probably best to consult him as soon as possible after detecting signs of mouth rot or any problem requiring antibiotic remedies.

At times you may discover that your pet's eyes are swollen or infected. Seepage may have caused the eyes to become sealed shut. If this is the case, your animal may have a bacterial infection because it has become too cold or has been subjected to drafts. Your veterinarian may suggest heat treatments or antibiotic eye ointments with a supplement of multivitamins.

If your pet iguana has watery eyes or the eyes appear sunken, if its coloring is dull and gray, and if it refuses to eat, it may be suffering from a respiratory disease. Since iguanas hail from tropical climates, they are extremely susceptible to such threatening respiratory disorders. Early symptoms of respiratory problems are difficulty in breathing, sneezing, nasal discharges, continual saliva drainage from the mouth, loss of appetite, and a general lethargic attitude. Respiratory diseases are often fatal and should be dealt with immediately by your veterinarian, who will probably inject oxytetracycline or a similar antibiotic. Injections should be continued, with a supplement of 100 mg of antibiotic powder every day, until the animal shows marked improvement or is completely cured.

The head is a good place to check for early signs of ill health. Look at the eyes, are they watery? How about the mouth, does it close all the way? Are the gums swollen? And the nostrils, do they have any mucus running out of them? You should perform such cursory inspections at least every two weeks. Photo by W. P. Mara.

Do not handle the animal any more than absolutely necessary except for the administration of medication. The less it is handled, the less stressful it will feel. Make certain the animal is receiving some direct sunlight or ultraviolet light. Maintain a warm temperature of 82°–90°F both day and night. Keep the animal's cage antiseptically clean, rinsing it often to make sure no chemicals remain. If your iguana goes off its food, try varying the animal's diet and offer it food more often. Do not try to force it to eat. Consult your veterinarian, who may suggest a penicillin or other antibiotic injection.

If you've acquired your animal from a pet shop, you will probably be able to fill in its medical history. It is extremely important to carefully examine *any* pet you are about to bring into your home to make certain that health problems or potential health problems do not exist—for *your* sake as well as the animal's.

55

BREEDING
IGUANAS

Since it is extremely difficult to get iguanas to breed in captivity, they are not usually recommended to pet owners who have their hearts set on attempting to breed a larger pet stock. In the past many pet texts have stated that the animals *will not* breed in captivity. However, in more recent years there have been more and more reported successes in breeding the animals away from their natural habitats. It is not our intention to dissuade any potential pet owner from trying his or her hand at breeding iguanas. While breeding the animals is very difficult, we feel it is important to present the details of the process to illustrate some of the obstacles as well as to show that it is no longer considered "impossible."

In the wild and even in larger cages, male iguanas are extremely territorial. This is very evident during their breeding season. It is at this time that ritualistic fights occur between the males. They raise themselves up on all fours and threateningly display their spread dewlap. A common iguana "battle" will begin with the animals slowly circling one another. Once they come face-to-face, they will thrash their heads together until one gives up and departs or submissively presses its body to the ground. The winner of this "battle" will be content to let the loser escape. At times, if the other male is submissive, the dominate iguana will allow it to remain in his territory, knowing that it poses no threat to its mating desires.

Opposite: Getting iguanas to breed in captivity is a difficult undertaking, but it is no longer considered impossible.

Female iguanas are not nearly so aggressive even during the mating season. They will fight over nesting places if good ones are limited, but otherwise they ignore one another.

During copulation the male secures a grip on the female's neck or head with his teeth while grasping the female's tail with one of his hind legs. The male sways his head from side to side. Copulation lasts anywhere from one to 20 minutes. The gestation period is from 49 to 90 days.

Green iguanas are hatched from eggs that are laid in burrows in sandy earth, usually near a body of water. The burrow is normally anywhere from three to six feet long and about two feet below the surface. Approximately a week prior to lay-

One of the few times female iguanas come down from the trees is during the mating season.

ing her eggs, the female will stop eating and will slowly increase her intake of water until water is all she appears to exist upon.

The female will lay her clutch over about a five-hour period. A normal clutch of iguana eggs can number as many as 30, laid two at a time. The interval between the laying of each pair of eggs increases over the five hours. As do many other female lizards, female iguanas store sperm until the time they actually lay their eggs. In the wild the eggs are laid around February, with hatching beginning in April and May during the rainy season. The eggs are about 1½ inches long and have a diameter of about one inch. They weigh less than a third of an ounce each. All of the eggs hatch at about the same time.

The young iguanas hatch out on their own, with no aid from their parents. They measure about eight inches long at birth and are natural swimmers. They will instinctively burrow to the surface. The young iguanas will live in the low brush vegetation and will hunt for food together. They often sleep on top of one another. This may be for warmth or for protection or both. Sexual maturity is reached, depending on the individual animal, between two and three years of age.

In 1984 the Smithsonian Institution reported a major success in breeding iguanas in captivity. However, their success was part of a program designed to study the feasibility of raising iguanas on either large or small farms or ranches in order to mass produce them as a Latin American food source. They cited some of the same problems pet exporters have noted, such as the dwindling iguana population due to overhunting and the continual development (i.e., destruction) of the animal's natural habitat.

While a pet owner might find the idea of eating an iguana repugnant, the problems the Smithsonian met and overcame while tackling this project are of interest regardless of the eventual use of the animal in question, whether as pet or food.

The Smithsonian researchers reported that the hundreds of wild-born iguana hatchlings they had in captivity grew as fast or faster than their wild counterparts even with only a half square yard of individual living space. Hatchling iguanas in the wild risk nearly a 90% mortality rate, but, because of the

lack of predators, the Smithsonian iguanas enjoyed close to 100% survival. This tends to support what pet owners have long observed: the iguana takes well to captivity, becoming more docile the longer it remains a pet.

Beginning with about 400 hatchlings captured from nest sites in their natural habitats, the researchers built a number of 12-square-yard enclosures in a Panamanian national park. Within these they constructed hiding boxes from natural vegetation and bamboo, providing the same thick sunning perches pet owners make sure their pets are provided. They placed ten to 20 hatchlings in each enclosure. These were fed diets identical to those suggested for pets. The hatchlings did so well that the researchers increased the enclosure populations to 60 animals each.

After this step proved so successful, the Smithsonian researchers captured a number of pregnant iguanas and provided them with an enclosure that included an open clearing, the iguana's favorite type of nesting site. Their plan was to let them lay their eggs, then dig them up and attempt artificial incubation. The problem they encountered was that the females created complex tunneling systems to protect their eggs. Even after digging out the entire tunneling system, the researchers often could not find the clutch of eggs. They overcame this by building their own artificial egg chambers and burying them in the site. Luckily, the female iguanas utilized them and the researchers were able to collect hundreds of eggs.

The eggs were put in plastic containers with dirt, and the containers were in turn placed in a plywood box. The temperature was carefully maintained and the eggs periodically weighed and measured. The researchers reported that over 700 iguanas hatched from this artificial incubation method.

If you hope to have your animals breed, you naturally have to have a pair of the opposite sex. You may need the aid of your pet shop manager in sexing a pair of iguanas since expert examination is the first step in determining which is which. Generally the males are larger and have larger dewlaps under their throats and more pronounced dorsal spines. The males also have brighter coloring than the females. The brighter coloring of the male attracts predators toward the male and away

The male iguana displays its dewlap to intimidate rival males and to impress females.

from the female and also serves a purpose in defining territories and fending off competitors.

Since they are reluctant to breed in captivity, your iguanas have to live in conditions as close to their natural habitat as possible. The larger the terrarium, the more chance there is of the two mating.

The female stores the male's sperm, fertilization of the eggs occurring in her oviducts before the eggs become encapsulated in their shells. Since females store sperm, there is always a chance that a clutch of eggs laid long after mating is still fertile. Keep a careful watch on her after she begins to refuse food and take in increasingly larger amounts of water. This is an indication that she is about to lay her eggs. The previously pregnant female will normally return to a favorite spot after having abandoned it to find a nesting place. The only sign that the female has laid her eggs may be her suddenly slender or even emaciated appearance. When any of these things are observed, it is time to start looking for the clutch.

Part of the reason that iguanas have a high mortality rate in the wild is because of their eggs are often eaten before they are hatched. In your terrarium they will probably survive,

but there is always a chance that the eggs will be eaten by animals being used as food (mealworms, mice) or even by the parent iguanas themselves. Once discovered, the eggs can be dug up and transferred to a specially constructed incubator. Before picking up the eggs, carefully mark the top of each one and place it in its exact original position in the brood container. This is done so that the developing embryo inside is not damaged by repositioning of the egg. Many keepers now believe that turning a lizard egg once or twice does no damage, but why take a chance.

One type of incubator is a plastic container measuring about 18 by 10 by 12 inches and lined with bricks on the bottom. The bricks are covered with about three inches of water and a water heater with a thermostat is placed in the water. A thermostat is suspended in the water from a wire insert on which rests another plastic container with a suitable substrate. This second container is where the eggs rest. A glass panel is fitted at an angle over the second container to help maintain humidity. The entire incubator is covered with a ventilated plastic lid. The eggs will rapidly increase in size due to their absorption of moisture.

The inner egg container should measure about 8 by 8 by 2 inches and should contain a sterilized peat moss and sand mixture or vermiculite. Sterilization can be done by simply boiling the peat moss mixture prior to placing it in the container. By maintaining a temperature of between 77° and 94°F, the humidity within such an incubator will remain between 90% and 100% even with a ventilated lid.

Upon hatching after some 110-120 days, the young iguana will poke its snout out of the shell but may not emerge completely for several hours. It forcefully rotates its body until the shell separates and the little lizard (some eight to 11 inches long) is freed. Because of improper care, poor parental diet, or incubation temperatures either too high or too low, a baby iguana may be too weak to emerge on its own. You may have to cut the egg shell and separate it from the animal with the use of forceps. It is important that the nostrils of the newborn be cleared immediately so that it can breathe properly. Even with this rescue, it is unlikely that young animals too weak to

Iguanas become sexually mature at about two to three years of age.

hatch on their own will survive for very long outside the shell.

After a number of the iguanas have hatched, you can begin transferring them to their permanent home in small groups. Make sure they are provided with places to sun themselves and places where they can hide. After about ten days, the yolk sac remnants will be consumed and the animals will have to seek out their first solid foods. On occasion the young iguanas will seek out food together, but once they find something to eat they will not share it with the others. They do not appear to rely on others of their kind for any sort of companionship. They will appear to totally ignore one another, often crowding together on a perch. Remember, the young iguanas need more meat in their diets than do their parents. They will slowly change to the vegetable diet as they age.

Iguanas learn very slowly and have little retention. They will follow sunlight around their cage, but this is due to the instinctive behavior of seeking warmth rather than any measure of intelligence.

They will reach their sexual maturity after two to three years. As they mature, the iguanas will become increasingly docile and more and more like their parents. As they grow, their diet and other requirements change to reflect the needs of the adult iguana.

INDEX